Truelove Hills

The Matchmaker

PATRINA McKENNA

Copyright © 2020 Patrina McKenna

All rights reserved

This book is a work of fiction. Names, characters, places, and incidents either are products of the author's imagination or are used fictitiously. Any resemblance to actual persons, living or dead, events, or locales is entirely coincidental.

Publisher: Patrina McKenna

patrina.mckenna@outlook.com

ISBN-13: 978-0-9932624-7-0

Also by Patrina McKenna

The **GIANT Gemstones** *series*

Feel good fantasy for the whole family!

GIANT Gemstones
A Galaxy of Gemstones
The Gemstone Dynasty
Enrico's Journey
Summer Camp at Tadgers Blaney Manor

The **Truelove Hills** *series*

Romantic comedy with a twist!

Truelove Hills
Truelove Hills – Mystery at Pebble Cove
Truelove Hills – The Matchmaker

DEDICATION

For my family and friends

PROLOGUE

David Makepeace scratched his head before folding the handwritten note and placing it on the sideboard. What a load of nonsense. His first thought was that one of the regulars in the pub had written it; maybe someone who had been rebuffed by the twins. Strange though that the note had been slipped under the door of his private apartment at the Solent Sea Guest House that evening. Anyone could have done it; the guest house door was always unlocked until eleven in the evenings. It was the first job he did after closing time at the King Arthur public house next door.

It was now almost midnight and David yawned before opening the bottom drawer of the sideboard and shoving the note under a load of papers he kept when he felt they shouldn't be thrown away. He wasn't one for keeping a precise filing system. Within ten minutes his head sank into his goose feather pillow – a present from his daughter, Matilda, last Christmas. He always fell straight asleep after sinking his nose into the welcome softness at the end of a long day – but not tonight.

His mind stirred a while still taking in the content of the note:

The twins are in trouble.

The more David thought about it; he knew it was a prank. Come to think of it; it was probably the twins themselves trying to get attention. They'd always been trouble, those two. David smiled as he recalled some of Tabitha and Tallulah's many escapades before turning over and giving the note no further thought.

1

THE GIG RACE

It was the first Friday in August, and the long-awaited beach party was planned for tonight. Matilda closed the door to Villa Tressler and headed the short distance across the pebblestone lane to Villa Summer next door carrying seven-month-old Mollie on her hip. Her best friend, Cindy, had volunteered to provide the catering for tonight's event and Matilda was keen to help. Jamie rushed out of Villa Summer and down the steps carrying one-year-old Sebastian.

'Hi, Tilly! Must dash. Need to drop Sebastian off at nursery before driving to the heliport. Tristan is flying me to London for a meeting this morning. I'll be back in time for the gig race later. There's no way Theo's boat will beat mine – he's got Tallulah in his team, and we all know how unpredictable she is, she missed both of the training sessions. We only gave her a place to make up the numbers. We were one man down.'

Cindy leant out of an upstairs window of Villa Summer. 'Don't take any notice of him, Tilly. Anyone would think it's a professional race – they're only doing it for fun! Come in; I'll be down in a minute. I can't wait to give Mollie a cuddle. She looks so cute in that sun hat.'

Jamie winked over the top of Sebastian's turquoise cap, which matched the colour of both father and son's eyes to perfection. 'Trust me, Tilly, Gig Sonning-Smythe will be soaring through the sea like a dream come six o'clock. Gig Tressler will be limping along letting in water!'

Matilda sat on the sofa and marvelled at her friend's energy. Apart from owning and working in the bakery, delicatessen and bistro in the village, Cindy's home was always spotless. All Matilda could do these days, was look after Mollie and keep an eye on the temporary staff who were running her gift shop. Still, Mollie was the most important thing and Matilda couldn't quite bring herself to leave her at Little Finchies & Friends nursery yet. Maybe in a couple of months she'd go back to work on a part-time basis. She was lucky to have the option – Truelove Hills was now a booming holiday destination and Matilda's husband,

Theo, as Head of Tourism was being well rewarded for the success. It was hard to believe that just two years ago, the picturesque village lay dormant in an undiscovered part of southern England.

Mollie giggled as Cindy lifted her high in the air and spun around with her. Matilda sat with her hands in her lap, feeling insignificant. She sighed and managed her best smile before standing up and taking Mollie back from her friend. 'I've just popped round to see if you need any help with the catering for tonight.'

Cindy plumped up the cushions on the sofa as she spoke, 'It's all sorted, Tilly. The staff in the bistro have ordered in extra provisions, and I'm closing it for this evening so that they can all come down to the beach. They'll be supervising the hog roast and barbecue, on the promise of normal wages and free beer. Your father's taken on temporary staff at the pub tonight to release Steve, Bruce and Tallulah to take part in the gig race and Toby Finchinglake is setting up a wine marquee. Tabitha's lined up to help with that.'

Cindy rushed into the hallway and pulled a lip gloss out of her pocket before viewing her reflection in a large ornate mirror. 'Do you think this colour is too peach? I usually go for pink?'

Matilda stood behind her friend and was shocked to see her own reflection. Cindy's shiny blonde hair was tied in a neat ponytail, her blue eyes sparkled, and she glowed. There was no other word for it; Cindy positively glowed. In comparison, Matilda's long wavy brown hair was in desperate need of a trim, her large blue eyes were half-hidden under her fringe, and her smile was forced.

'What do you think, too peach or not?'

A switch flicked at Matilda's very core. 'Definitely too peach, go back to pink. Well done with having everything in control for tonight. Must dash, I've got such a busy day ahead. See you later on the beach.'

First stop for Matilda was Little Finchies & Friends. With the village in need of a nursery, Toby Finchinglake had sourced a property and funded the development and Hannah, Matilda's eldest sister – a lawyer and Toby's fiancée – had recruited the staff. The nursery manager, Miss Mae, was jovial, plump and in her forties. Cindy and Jamie had been raving about the benefit of Sebastian mixing with other little ones, and Miss Mae had taken it upon herself to become a part of the community. Matilda and Mollie had bumped into her on lots of occasions; in Matilda's shop, the King Arthur public house and Cindy's Bakery to name but a few. Mollie always smiled, and high-fived Miss Mae.

'I know this is very short notice, Miss Mae, but could I book Mollie into the nursery today?'

Miss Mae performed an impromptu jig in the middle of the nursery floor, and Mollie raised her arms squealing with delight. 'There's always room for Mollie. Mr Finchinglake has kindly provided more staff than we need. Some days there are more staff than children. The more little ones, the merrier, that's what I always say!'

Matilda handed Mollie over to Miss Mae and jogged back to Villa Tressler to make some phone calls. Somehow over the last seven months (and being hospitalised for two months before Mollie was born), Matilda had lost her spirit.

Theo arrived home just before five o'clock to a note from his wife:

Darling Theo,

If you get home before me can you please pick Mollie up from the nursery? I've gone into town to have my hair cut and to buy some new clothes. I can hear you say 'about time'!

Sorry for being a frump. Thanks for putting up with me for so long without moaning. If you see Cindy, please ask if I can borrow her peach lip gloss (that'll shock her).

I'm really looking forward to tonight and will be cheering on Team Tressler in the gig race.

Love you lots, Tilly xxx

By six o'clock the gig crews were in place. Matilda wasn't back, and Theo handed Mollie over to Hannah. 'Should I be worried, Hannah? This is very out of character for Tilly.'

Hannah tried to reassure her brother-in-law. 'Just focus on the race, Theo. It's about time my sister had a day to herself. She'll be all the better for it. I'm sure she'll be back soon.'

Team Tressler's cox raised an arm to signify his boat was ready to race. Theo scanned the shoreline for Hannah and Mollie and was relieved to see Matilda running down the beach. She looked amazing. Her wavy hair was now shoulder length and clipped up on one side with white flowers. Her cobalt blue maxi dress matched her eyes, and she was waving both arms in the air to attract Theo's attention. Theo was stunned by the transformation. He smiled broadly and waved back.

Jamie was having a last rallying talk with his team before signifying to his cox to raise his arm too. The race was to Pebble Point and back; a large rock formation 1.5 kilometres from the shoreline at high tide.

Lord Sonning-Smythe checked his stopwatch and nodded to Arthur Makepeace, who pursed his lips before releasing an ear-piercing whistle. The gigs were off! The spectators lined the shoreline with plastic glasses in hand. Tabitha was more of a cider girl but, after offering to help in the Finchinglake Vineyard marquee, she thought she should sample the different wines on offer. She stood on the beach swaying to the music when her favourite song came through the sound system. Tabitha took another sip of wine and decided to be daring. Her twin sister, Tallulah, always took the limelight. She'd done it again today by being the only girl rowing in the race.

Tabitha's eyes fell on the megaphone that Lord Sonning-Smythe, "Clive" to people who knew him, was using earlier to announce the rowers. She slipped off her flipflops, grabbed the megaphone and climbed onto one of the wooden tables near the currently unsupervised hog roast. The crowd were cheering on Theo and Jamie's teams and oblivious that Tabitha was now standing tall behind them. The gigs had rounded Pebble Point and were on their way back to shore. There wasn't much in it as far as Tabitha could see from her elevated position. She flicked back her long curly red hair, and her emerald eyes sparkled behind her sunglasses. There was half of the song left and, for once in her life, Tabitha was going to take the attention away from Tallulah.

First, there was an irritating buzzing noise which grew louder and turned into a whirring sound. The cheering crowd didn't hear it. Tabitha removed her sunglasses, looked up the coast in the direction of the noise, and shouted into the megaphone: 'STOP THE

RACE!'

The crowd turned around, and the rowers looked up. Tabitha was never one to cause a fuss; everyone was shocked. Tabitha pointed north up the coast. 'SPEEDBOAT APPROACHING FROM PEBBLE COVE. STOP ROWING NOW!'

The gigs bobbed about in the sea with all eyes on the approaching speedboat. It shot past, causing both boats to capsize.

Arthur turned to Clive. 'Well, I never, Leticia Lovett's bought a speedboat.'

Clive raised his eyebrows. 'The Lady certainly has. Even with that headscarf and dark glasses, she was instantly recognisable – her butler was in the driving seat.' Clive looked over at the sodden rowers carrying their gigs back to shore. 'I suggest we call the race a draw and get the barbecue lit. Your granddaughter is quite the heroine.'

Arthur smiled to himself and glanced over at Tabitha, Matilda and Hannah, helping a drenched Tallulah onto the beach. As far as he was concerned, all of his granddaughters were heroines.

2

THE MISSING NECKLACE

Tallulah had searched everywhere. She had treasured the silver chain with a sparkly charm of the Eiffel Tower since she bought it with her first wages for doing a paper round at the Post Office & General Store, aged thirteen. She remembered that day well. Her boss, Mrs Carruthers, had erected a table next to the Post Office counter and asked for bric-a-brac items she could sell for charity. Tallulah had been keeping an eye on the donated items and was the first to see the necklace. Tallulah handed back her wage packet and begged Mrs Carruthers to sell it to her. Mrs Carruthers raised a wiry grey eyebrow and suppressed a smile. That girl was never short in asking for anything. Having said that, she was a good worker, and Mrs Carruthers admired her spirit, so she took two pounds out of the wage packet and handed the remaining wages back to Tallulah along with the necklace.

Tallulah had never owned anything so beautiful, and she viewed it as a good luck charm. She rarely wore it – only when she needed a bit of help, like her final exams at art school in London and yesterday's gig race – and now she couldn't find it.

The cleaners in the King Arthur had alerted David Makepeace to his daughter's ransacked room. He ran his fingers through his black curly hair when he saw the mess and his green eyes narrowed as Tallulah entered.

David turned to face his daughter. 'Have we been burgled or do I need to discipline you for letting your room get into such a state?'

Tallulah lowered her long black lashes and raised a hand to touch the empty space around her neck. 'I've lost my lucky charm and, as it's not in my room, I've come to the conclusion that it's at the bottom of the ocean since the gig race that got scuppered by Lady Leticia Lovett and her butler on that flipping speedboat. By the way, she looked ridiculous, wearing a scarf and dark glasses. I have a good mind to go up to Chateau Amore de Pebblio and ask her to fund the trawling of the sea bed, or at least buy me a new necklace.'

David raised an eyebrow. 'Is there anywhere else

you could have lost it?'

Tallulah rubbed her forehead. 'I don't know! I've been everywhere around the village. I work in the pub, I cover for Mrs Carruthers in the Post Office & General Store on more than one occasion each week, I pick AJ up from school for Hannah when she's doing her law work, I'm always taking Fluffy for walks up to Pebble Peak as it's a bit of a climb for Grandpa these days, and Cindy keeps asking me to collect Sebastian from nursery when she's running late.' Tallulah folded her arms and stamped her foot. 'Come to think of it – I'm the village dogsbody!'

David took a couple of steps backwards; he was going to ask Tallulah if she could work both Saturday and Sunday in the pub as Bruce Copperfield was taking his new girlfriend away for the weekend. His heart sank – people were certainly leaning on Tallulah, and he knew it didn't stop there – they were using Tabitha too. He released a slow sigh. The twins were twenty-three now. Their elder sisters, Hannah and Matilda, had families and lives of their own and Tabitha and Tallulah were stuck at home helping him run the pub.

It was at times like this that David missed his beloved Harriet. If the girls had a mother, she would know what to do. He was definitely out of his comfort zone; all he could do was hope for the best as far as the twins were concerned and turn his mind back to running his businesses. *He'd* need to cover for Bruce this weekend; he wouldn't ask Tallulah to help out on this occasion.

Tallulah glanced at her watch. 'Oh, for goodness sake, I'm late now to look after Mollie this morning. Tilly's going into her shop for a few hours to do a stocktake. Must dash!'

*

The village gift shop – Matilda's Memorabilia – was a hive of activity. The two job-share temporary staff had taken it easy while Matilda had been on maternity leave but, to their dismay, she was now a rejuvenated version of her former self and asking too many questions for their liking. They had both been called in at short notice for a whole day stocktake, and their boss was holding no prisoners. By the end of the day, they had both been fired.

*

Matilda stirred the pasta while Theo settled Mollie into her cot. The sound of soft footsteps down the stairs was a sign of success and, within seconds, Theo's arms wrapped around Matilda's waist, his unshaven face snagging her freshly styled hairdo. 'I can't believe I've got my wife back, and with such a quick turnaround. Yesterday the makeover, and today the back to work businesswoman. Are you sure Mollie's going to be OK with Miss Mae at the nursery? It'll be quite a change for her.'

Matilda drained the pasta then added it to the sauce. 'Mollie loves Miss Mae. There's something special about that woman. I don't know how the village managed without her before. She's only been here a few months, and apart from getting the nursery up and running, she's fast becoming an integral member of the community. I think some of her energy's rubbed off on me!'

Theo carried the pasta bowls into the garden and placed them on the pale blue tablecloth that matched the painted shutters of Villa Tressler. He breathed in the sea air and raised the pastel pink parasol to bring shade from the evening sun. Theo smiled at the sight of the large shells they had collected from the beach, which were now being used to hold down the tablecloth from the slight sea breeze. He sniffed the bowl of floating flowers and candles his wife had arranged in the centre of the table and closed his eyes to count his blessings. Buying one of Clive's Sea View Villas and living there with his wife and child had been a dream too far away from wishing when he worked in London. What a difference two years had made. His new life in Truelove Hills was blissful.

Matilda unfolded her napkin. 'Forgot to mention. Tallulah's on the warpath. She's lost her Eiffel Tower necklace, and she's holding Lady Lovett to blame for the boating accident yesterday.'

Theo blew on his forkful of pasta. 'Well, she's certainly picked the wrong person to have a fight with. Leticia Lovett will eat her alive, spit her out and ban her from ever visiting Chateau Amore de Pebblio again and that would be a pity.'

'Why would it be a pity?'

'Because I've just been given notice that Leticia's hosting another matchmaking event at the chateau and she gave me a nod and a wink to get Tabitha and Tallulah to participate this time. She says the twins could do with some romance in their lives.'

Matilda raised her eyebrows. 'Well, that's very thoughtful of her and quite out of character! I'll smooth things over with Tallulah. There's a pretty silver necklace in the shop with a shamrock charm encrusted with emeralds. Miss Mae suggested that it would suit Tallulah. Let's hope she prefers it to the Eiffel Tower charm.'

Theo reached across the table to squeeze Matilda's hand. 'Great idea. I've never known a girl to turn down emeralds.'

Matilda snatched her hand back. 'How many girls have you given emeralds to?'

Theo threw his head back and laughed, flashing his white teeth and enhancing his dimples. 'None! Now, if you ask Jamie next door the same question, I doubt you'd get the same answer.'

It was now Matilda's turn to chuckle before winking. 'Don't you mention that to Cindy!'

3

FRIENDS REUNITED

From the balcony of Villa Summer, there was a sweeping view of the coastline heading south. There was also a good view of the Sea View Villas that Jamie's father, Clive, owned and which Theo marketed for him as part of the Truelove Hills experience.

Cindy sat on the balcony painting her nails as Matilda practised different styles with her shortened wavy brown hair. 'What do you think, Cindy? At least I can still tie it up when I need to.'

'It looks great, Tilly! I can't remember when we last had a girls' night in. I've missed you since you became Mollie's mum.'

Matilda laughed. 'I've missed me too. I'm back now, though. I can't believe how quickly Mollie's settled into Little Finchies & Friends. Miss Mae's an absolute godsend.'

Cindy replaced the lid on the bottle of nail varnish and waved her fingers in the air. 'We're so lucky to have a new nursery in the village. Toby Finchinglake has been more than generous with the funding. Has Hannah set their wedding date yet? Will they hold it at Finchinglake Vineyard or go for Chateau Amore de Pebblio like we did?'

Matilda's large blue eyes widened further. 'I've been so lost in my own world that I've totally neglected my sisters. I'll arrange to meet Hannah for coffee later in the week. I should make more of an effort with Tabitha and Tallulah too. I'm forever asking favours and giving nothing back. I'm just rubbish, aren't I?'

Cindy sensed Matilda's mood dipping. 'No, you're not. I think you all need a good chin-wag and a bit of a treat. Why don't you come to the bistro on Monday evening? I'm sure your dad will give Tabitha and Tallulah time off from the pub – Monday's are always quiet. If you can get Theo to look after Mollie, I'll make sure Jamie's home in time to bath Sebastian. Knowing our husbands, they'll probably double up on the babysitting front and have their own party! I can easily cook a three-course meal for four *and* do the waitressing. It'll be my pleasure, and I promise not to listen in on any gossip.'

Matilda jumped up and hugged her friend. Cindy held her arms out wide to protect her nails and knocked a pot plant off the balcony into the garden below. Both friends leant over to assess the damage. The pink geranium had become uprooted, and potting compost was strewn over the patio.

Cindy grinned. 'No harm done. Good job it was a plastic pot. My nails are just about dry, I'd best go down and sweep it up, or Jamie will think I've been drinking on the balcony again. Now, there's a thought. Why *aren't* we drinking? I'll bring some prosecco up on my way back. I need a treat as I'll be working on Monday night now. You just stay right there and admire the view until I get back.'

Matilda leant on the balcony. It was getting dark, and Cindy flicked on the outside floodlight to ensure she brushed away all evidence of the fallen pot plant. She sent a thumbs-up sign and winked before disappearing back into the house and turning the floodlight off. Matilda stretched over the right-hand corner of the balcony to peer into Villa Tressler next door. Theo was in the kitchen, and the light in Mollie's nursery was off. Everything was quiet in Villa Summer too, so the falling pot plant hadn't disturbed Sebastian, who was sleeping in a room down the corridor. Matilda felt a sense of calm wash over her as she took in the view of the twinkling lights along the seafront, and the warm glow coming from a bedroom window of Villa Veronique.

A car's headlights lit up the pebblestone lane below and Matilda watched as the family renting Villa Julianna for two weeks returned to their accommodation after a day's outing.

Cindy returned with the prosecco. 'All sorted. Jamie will never know the difference. I'll have it re-potted and back on the balcony before he gets home later.'

Matilda helped herself to the bowl of peanuts Cindy had brought up on the tray. 'I see Miss Mae's out again tonight; there are no lights on in Villa Elena. I wonder if she'll buy a property rather than renting, or even rent something smaller? It'll be costing her a fortune to rent a four-bedroom villa. Clive must be thrilled to have a long-term booking at one of his properties. I see Villa Veronique's occupied too.'

Cindy shook her head and gulped her prosecco before reaching for the nuts. 'Villa Veronique's vacant this week.'

Matilda stood up and surveyed the three rental villas. 'That's strange, I thought that too, but there was a bedroom light on earlier.'

Cindy reached for more nuts. 'It'll be on a timer. Clive's a stickler for security. Anyway, did I mention that Miss Mae is fast becoming my top customer at the bakery? She pops in for croissants and Danish pastries every morning and has a regular order for sandwiches, pasties and cakes at lunchtime for the staff at Little Finchies & Friends. Now, there's a thought, it hadn't crossed my mind before; do you think Toby Finchinglake has named the nursery "Little Finchies & Friends" because he wants a few little Finchinglakes? He hasn't got children of his own, has he? I know he's a great father to AJ, Hannah did well to secure a ring on her finger from him – a father for AJ and a vineyard to boot, not to mention a fortune he's inherited in emeralds! He's a bit older than her though. Nearly forty? What's Hannah now? Thirty-one? It won't surprise me if six-year-old AJ has a little brother or sister soon.'

Matilda topped up her glass and took a slurp. Even with Cindy, she didn't like gossiping about her sisters. However, Cindy had a point. 'He is rather dishy, isn't he – Toby Finchinglake? Now, I wouldn't swap Theo for the world, but those silver eyes, mass of light brown hair *and* his own vineyard and family fortune are rather attractive, aren't they?'

Cindy stretched her arms above her head and nodded. 'Definitely. But your Theo has dimples to die for. You've done well, my girl. Now when it comes to

Jamie; he's the only one for me. I knew it from the day he came into my bakery. Tanned, turquoise eyes, dark blonde hair. He's a younger version of his father and, apart from the tan, an older version of his son. But the thing that stood out most for me was his expensive aftershave; Truelove Hills had never been subjected to such an aroma ever before!'

The girls giggled, they were back together, the best friends there could be. Having a bit of a gossip under the influence of prosecco worked wonders for the soul.

*

The occupant of Villa Veronique sent a text message:

I'M IN PLACE.

OPERATION DOUBLE G UNDERWAY.

ASSUME YOUR POSITIONS.

COUNTDOWN TWO WEEKS.

4

SISTERLY CATCH-UP

It was Monday night, and Cindy's Bistro was open for a private party. Tallulah wore the emerald shamrock charm on a silver chain around her neck and Tabitha glared at Matilda. 'What I want to know is why my twin gets to receive an expensive necklace, and I get nothing. I was the one who stopped the gig race and, in the process, eliminated any casualties.'

Tabitha folded her arms and Matilda could see her point. 'I know you two insist you're treated equally, so I'll find a necklace for you in the shop tomorrow. Luckily, Toby is still keeping us supplied with emeralds; he has a never-ending source. That man is kind beyond all measure.'

Everyone looked at a blushing Hannah and Matilda grabbed her hand. 'You're so lucky to have found

Toby; his generosity knows no bounds. We're so grateful for the nursery he's funded, how's the after-school club coming along?'

Hannah wiped her brow and took a gulp of water. 'Oh, you know Toby. Always doing his best for other people.'

Tallulah looked at Tabitha before they both lowered their eyes; Hannah was in some sort of a strop with Toby. Cindy arrived with a tray of antipasti. 'Enjoy, everyone! Shout if you need any more drinks, I'll just be out back in the kitchen.'

Cindy hovered by the kitchen door keeping an eye on the tuna, olive and tomato sauce while the linguine cooked on a timer. Matilda had her work cut out tonight. Hannah was remote, and the twins were miffed about their unequal treatment of necklaces.

The main course served; Matilda asked the burning question. 'Well, Hannah, you've been engaged to Toby for months now. When do we need to book a date to look for bridesmaid dresses?'

Hannah put her fork down on her uneaten pasta. 'There's no need.' Cindy nudged nearer to the kitchen door. The dessert was in the fridge, so she was free to listen in. The sisters, apart from Hannah, ate the main course in silence. Hannah just stared into thin air.

Cindy cleared the plates and locked eyes with

Matilda. Matilda's soul shrank. Hannah and Toby had split up, could things get any worse? What would happen to AJ? Her curly-haired lovable nephew didn't know who his birth father was, and neither did Hannah. AJ doted on Toby; they were a perfect match. Now his world was about to come crashing down. Matilda's eyes filled with tears and Tabitha and Tallulah didn't raise theirs.

Cindy couldn't bear it any longer. She brought out a tray full of Limoncello sorbets and dragged a chair over from a nearby table. 'We're all here for you, Hannah. I'm not a sister in blood, but we all grew up together, and whenever there's a crisis we pull together as one unit. You are an intelligent, strong woman. You lived in Dubai on your own and hid AJ from us all for four years, for goodness sake. If you've now split up with Toby, it's not the end of the world. You're an esteemed lawyer. You have us. We can all help out. No man is worth the pain.'

Tabitha offered consolation. 'We'd look rubbish in bridesmaid dresses anyway. We're getting too old for that.'

Tallulah's eyes flashed with defiance. 'You'll always be Hannah Makepeace. Hannah Finchinglake wouldn't have suited you.'

Hannah pushed away her Limoncello sorbet. 'You won't be my bridesmaids, and I'll not be changing my name, I'm a lawyer with my own business, I'll never change my name. I'm still Hannah Makepeace even though I got married two days ago to Toby.' Hannah's face was grey as she continued, 'I'm sorry, Cindy, for not eating anything, morning sickness is lasting all day with me.'

Tallulah raised her eyes. 'A shotgun wedding, well I never. Don't think you'll get away without some sort of party.'

Matilda hugged Hannah. 'Have you told Daddy and Grandpa? When's the baby due? I bet Toby's thrilled.'

'No, not yet, I'll tell them both tomorrow. You girls got the better of me. I just wish I could stop feeling so washed out. The baby's due in February and, yes, Toby's delighted. Well, he would be, *he* doesn't feel like a dishcloth that's been wrung out and left to dry.'

Tabitha chuckled. 'Oh, I'm sure it's not that bad. Once you're over the early stage, you'll be blooming.'

Cindy dashed behind the bar and emerged with a bottle of champagne. 'Sorry that you won't be able to drink this, Hannah, but *we* can. We need to have some sort of celebration!'

Hannah frowned. 'Please go ahead, don't mind me. Anyway, I should be really annoyed with you all for presuming that Toby and I had broken up. Why would you think that? Have I made a big mistake rushing into things?'

Tallulah sniggered; Hannah was really grouchy – pregnancy didn't suit her at all. Her usual "composed at all times" sister *was* human after all. They'd not seen her pregnant with AJ; thankfully they'd all been spared that pleasure.

Champagne poured; Cindy proposed a toast. 'To Hannah and Toby, a more perfect couple you could not wish to meet. Well done to Hannah for getting a ring on his finger so quickly. We'll just have to suffer the consequences of no wedding to attend, no bridesmaid dresses, no special day to light up our year. We'll all do that for you, Hannah, because we love you and we know that Toby won't let such a major event pass by without letting us share it at some stage. We can all wait for a big party. Raise your glasses everyone – to Hannah and Toby!'

The atmosphere had lifted from awkward to buoyant and the girls clinked glasses. 'To Hannah and Toby!'

Hannah smiled. 'Thank you everyone, that means a lot.'

Keen to divert the attention away from herself, Hannah turned to Matilda. 'Anyway, Tilly, I've been meaning to ask how you're getting on back at work. Is it a wrench leaving Mollie at the nursery?'

Matilda shook her head. 'I've never been so happy. I feel I have the right balance with everything. You did so well, recruiting Miss Mae and her team. The nursery is such a happy place. Mollie loves it.'

Cindy raised her glass in the air. 'I'll second that. Sebastian loves it there too. There's never any problem with dropping him off. He just runs in, now that he can walk of course. Before that, he'd have crawled there all the way from Villa Summer if we'd let him. I'm sure Miss Mae's some kind of Pied Piper. Where she gets all her energy from amazes me. She's always spinning the little ones around and doing jigs everywhere. We should find out what she eats for breakfast.'

Matilda looked over at Tallulah, whose shamrock charm necklace was catching the light. 'That reminds me. Remember the pebblestone pram Grandpa made for me when I was in hospital? The one with the emerald interior. You all know that it gave me a vision that I would be having a little girl. Well, it's on the windowsill in Mollie's nursery now, and I had another vision a few weeks ago.'

Cindy leant forward. 'Oh, do tell!'

Hannah twisted the emerald bracelet on her wrist; the one Toby had given to her soon after they first met. 'Well, I was once advised that emeralds are believed to foretell future events and reveal one's truths. Go on, Tilly, what did you see?'

'Only if you promise not to laugh.'

There was a chorus of: 'We won't laugh.'

'I saw Tallulah running through a field with a pint glass in her hand. It was a very green place.'

The room erupted with laughter. Tallulah spoke first. 'You've seen me loads of times rushed off my feet in the garden at the pub.'

Matilda rubbed her forehead. 'No, it wasn't a garden. It was definitely a field. A field with lots of trees.'

Sensing that her revelation was falling on deaf ears, Matilda decided to change the subject and share some tangible news. 'Now, don't go telling anyone until you hear officially, but Lady Leticia Lovett is holding another matchmaking event at the chateau, and she's going to invite Tabitha and Tallulah to take part.'

Tabitha clapped her hands. 'Ooooh, when?'

'The last weekend in August.'

Tallulah raised her eyes to the ceiling. 'I'd rather jog up to Pebble Peak every morning for a month than take part in one of Lady Leticia's staged affairs. Have you seen those girls going into the chateau on previous matchmaking events? All dressed up to the nine's, pulling designer cases, perfect hair and make-up? No way, will I be taking part.'

Hannah stood up. 'I'm sorry to spoil the party, girls, but I need to get an early night.'

Matilda hugged her. 'Of course, you do. Get as many early nights as you can before my little niece or nephew comes along. If I have a vision of whether it's a girl or a boy, do you want to know?'

There was a chorus of 'No!' and Hannah laughed. 'Take no notice of them, Tilly. I believe your visions stand for something. Didn't you think of telling fortunes in your shop at one stage?'

Tallulah scoffed. 'Don't encourage her. It's a load of old tosh if you ask me. Sorry, Tilly, but that's my honest opinion.'

Matilda laughed. 'We're all entitled to our own opinions. Don't worry; I'm not offended.'

Cindy waved to her friends and closed the door to the bistro. Well, that had been an eventful evening: Hannah married and pregnant; the twins being invited to a matchmaking event; and Matilda well and truly back to her usual self. Now, why was Tallulah running through a field with trees holding a pint glass? Cindy giggled; Tilly's imagination was beyond measure.

5

MATCHMAKING IN THE PLANNING

The last weekend in August had arrived, and Tabitha and Tallulah dragged their overnight bags up Truelove Hills High Street. Tallulah wore a baseball cap with a curly red ponytail threaded through the back and Tabitha wore her hair in a loose plait.

It wasn't easy manoeuvring the wheeled cases along the pebblestones, and Tallulah huffed all the way up the hill until they reached Chateau Amore de Pebblio. Tabitha pulled on the long rope on the right of the wooden arched doors, and within seconds they opened to the sight of Gerard the butler. 'Good morning to you both. Her Ladyship is waiting for you on the terrace. You may leave your bags in the courtyard, and I'll arrange for them to be taken to your rooms. Please follow me.'

Lady Leticia was sipping her morning cup of Earl

Grey tea and staring out to sea when the twins approached her. 'Oh, my goodness! Is that the time already? I was completely lost in my thoughts. It is paramount that this weekend goes to plan and that you are both betrothed by Monday evening. I have my reputation to think of.'

Tabitha whispered to Tallulah, 'Betrothed?'

Tallulah raised her eyes before whispering back, 'She means "engaged". Fat chance of that happening.'

Leticia gestured for the girls to sit down before she stood up and paced around the terrace, articulating her plan. 'I have held many matchmaking events at the chateau, but none as intricate as this. I have come to the conclusion that if I put all my efforts into just one or two eligible singles during the weekend, there will be a better success rate of sustainable relationships. With that in mind, instead of the usual mix of men and women of all ages, I have focused on you two entirely and identified twenty eligible bachelors for you to choose from. That should be enough, don't you agree?'

Tallulah struggled to control a fit of giggles, so Tabitha spoke for both of them. 'That's very kind of you, Lady Leticia. May I ask why you have decided to focus on us?'

Leticia lowered her eyes. 'You have both been brought to my attention as needing some motherly help. I don't have children, and neither does Miss Mae. It was, in fact, Miss Mae's suggestion that we could join forces and make your dreams come true.'

Tears welled in Tabitha's eyes, and Tallulah snorted behind her hand. 'How do you know what our dreams are?'

Tabitha elbowed her sister. 'Well, we're very grateful, Lady Leticia. Thank you for everything you're doing for us.'

Leticia snatched a sideways glance at Tallulah. The twins were identical in looks when Tallulah made the most of herself, but they were worlds apart in personality. Still, that wasn't a bad thing – there was little chance they'd both choose the same bachelor this weekend and the process should go swimmingly.

'Now, come along girls. Miss Mae's upstairs with the stylist. The hairdresser and make-up artist are due to arrive in ten minutes, and a selection of shoes was delivered yesterday from Louboutin and Jimmy Choo. The bachelors will arrive at four o'clock in time for afternoon tea on the terrace. Dinner will be served at eight for the top six bachelors.'

*

Who knew matchmaking could be such fun? After six hours of pampering, the twins were ready for afternoon tea. Not only were they ready for the first session, they had chosen evening dresses for dinner and outfits for the rest of the weekend. The stylist had departed, and the hairdresser and make-up artist remained on standby to ensure the girls looked their best at all times. They could only assume that Lady Leticia had been subjected to such privileged treatment when she was a young woman. It was a far cry from living above the pub next door to their father who had a private apartment in the guest house. With such elaborate clothes and make-up, the twins had stipulated just one condition of their own – no borrowed jewellery. They wanted to wear their new necklaces. Tallulah was becoming attached to her shamrock and Tabitha was now the proud owner of a silver palm tree with emerald encrusted leaves.

Miss Mae clapped her hands before squealing, 'I can't believe the transformation! You girls have blossomed into princesses during the course of a few hours. The bachelors will have trouble choosing between you. They won't be able to tell you apart.'

Tallulah scowled. How could that woman even suggest they needed transforming in the first place and – as for telling them apart – Tallulah was sure that wouldn't be a problem. The twins were as different in personality as a bottle of champagne and a can of coke. The men would see that straight away. Tallulah knew the confident, rich ones would make a beeline for her and Tabitha would attract the quieter types. That had always happened at school in Truelove Hills; in London when they were at art school and even now when they worked in their father's pub. Tallulah frowned, why was it then that they were both single? Tallulah's longest relationship had been with Cindy's brother, Bruce Copperfield, and Tabitha had enjoyed a short fling with a builder last year, but that had fizzled out. Come to think of it; Bruce Copperfield wasn't confident and rich – he was just mean and moody.

Afternoon tea was planned to take place on the terrace. There were four round tables, each with six chairs, with a selection of finger sandwiches and miniature pastries arranged in the centre. The finest bone china cups and saucers were displayed next to matching plates and crisp white linen serviettes. The twins surveyed the sight with Lady Leticia and Miss Mae. Tabitha was confused. 'Why are there twenty-four places set, when there are only twenty bachelors and two of us?'

Miss Mae was quick to answer. 'That's technically incorrect, my dear. There are twenty-eight places,' Miss Mae nodded to a rectangular table along the back wall, 'that's the top table over there.'

Tallulah snorted. 'Top table? It's not a wedding. Who's going to be sitting there?'

Lady Leticia sighed, Tallulah should be grateful for what she was doing to help her, not making fun of it.

Still, Tallulah was Tallulah, and if this weekend didn't find her a husband, then there was no hope. Remaining professional as always, Leticia reached up to check her blonde bun was still in place and took a deep breath before responding. 'Miss Mae and I will be joining you both at the top table. We will form a welcome line when the bachelors arrive and then take our seats before they take theirs. You will notice that we have clipboards on our chairs. Please remove before sitting and take with you when you join the bachelors at their tables throughout afternoon tea. You will spend fifteen minutes at each of the four tables, which are numbered one to four. Tallulah will start at Table 1, Tabitha at Table 4, then Tallulah will move to 2, 3 and 4 and Tabitha to 1, 2 and 3. That way you won't bump into one another, and things will run like clockwork.'

Tabitha felt a panic attack coming on. 'But how will we know when fifteen minutes is up? What are we supposed to write on the clipboards? Won't that look rude? Why have you both got clipboards too?'

Leticia placed her hand on Tabitha's arm. 'Take deep breaths, Tabitha. Calmness is key. Gerard will perform the role of Master of Ceremonies, and he will ring my late husband's cherished antique silver bell when it is time for you to move tables. You just need to remember which table you will be moving to. As for the clipboards, matchmaking is a business. We can leave nothing to chance. You will both need to make notes against the bachelors' names, or you will get confused with who's who. Miss Mae and I will be watching from afar to assess whether there is a whiff of chemistry in the air or a bad smell.'

Tallulah slapped a hand over her mouth. It was the only way to suppress a fit of giggles. Her eyes were watering, and she needed to get some air. She grabbed Tabitha's arm. 'If you will just excuse us, we should pop to the powder room before our guests arrive.'

Tallulah pushed Tabitha into the ladies' cloakroom and slammed the door shut before leaning on it then sliding to the floor, her pale-yellow floral dress billowing around her. 'I have never heard anything so ridiculous in my whole life! We're going to look stupid. I don't know about you, but the only way *I'm* going to get through this is by having fun.'

Tabitha pulled her sister up off the floor. 'It does all sound very wooden and not like us at all, but we haven't had any luck finding partners yet, so I'm willing to go along with things and see how it turns out. We've nothing to lose. Lady Leticia and Miss Mae have been very kind giving up their time like this. I feel a bit better now I know it's all so regimented. Gerard will be watching our every move so we won't be able to put a foot out of line.'

Tallulah blew her nose on some toilet paper and dabbed at her watery eyes. 'It's not just Gerard who'll be watching us – what's that all about "whiffs of chemistry" and "bad smells"? It cracks me up; it really does. If we end up becoming "betrothed" by the end of the weekend, it'll be a major miracle!'

6

AFTERNOON TEA

Miss Mae scrubbed through one name straight away. Apart from the fact the man had the weakest handshake she had ever come across, he had two missing teeth – right in the centre at the front. He said he'd lost them in a slight altercation. In her expert opinion, he was too weak to defend himself, let alone protect the twins. He didn't have the strength in those hands to get in a swift upper hook before getting punched in the mouth. Miss Mae had taken boxing lessons in her youth so she should know.

Lady Leticia was focused on one thing; those that looked the part. She could tell in the blink of an eye who was well-bred and who wasn't. She had a preference for inherited millionaires rather than self-made ones – conveniently forgetting the fact that her late husband bought Chateau Amore de Pebblio with the funds he'd accrued from his property business.

The silver bell, so cherished by Leticia's late husband, stood over four feet tall and was wheeled into the room on a trolley. When Gerard tapped it with a hammer, the sound reverberated throughout the village. So much so, that Mrs Carruthers from the Post Office & General Store and Arthur Makepeace, the twins' grandfather, took it upon themselves to carry deckchairs up the High Street and take up residence outside the chateau.

'Trust me, Arthur, there'll be lots of action a bit later on. If we sit here, then we will see all the comings and goings. Miss Mae said there were twenty bachelors, but only six would make it past afternoon tea.' Mrs Carruthers took her knitting out of her bag and handed Arthur a mint humbug. Arthur's little white dog, Fluffy, sat patiently in a begging position at Mrs Carruthers' feet, so she patted his head and gave him one too.

Inside the chateau, a giant of an Irishman, called Paddy, with shoulder-length black hair and sparkling blue eyes had captured Tallulah's attention. 'Now, Tallulah, is there a drop of Irish in you? Is there a reason you're wearing a shamrock?'

Tallulah touched her necklace. 'To be sure, I'm

from the Emerald Isle. You do believe me do you not?'

'Well, your emerald eyes are a match for any fair maiden's I've ever met.'

Tabitha was spoilt for choice. One of the bachelors had commented on her palm tree necklace and suggested he take her away on his yacht to somewhere exotic with real palm trees. Tabitha had pointed out that the south of England had palm trees in places. Her necklace was proving to be a real talking point. Miss Mae made a note of that for future reference.

The bell rang, and the twins changed tables. To be fair to Lady Leticia and Miss Mae, the event was turning out to be very well organised indeed. The clipboards were a godsend. The girls would have no way of remembering the individual characteristics of all the men otherwise. Tallulah made notes on Table 2: 'Not in my lifetime! … A double shift in the pub is more appealing … Bad teeth, hairy nose … Has potential … Wow!'

Tabitha's notes for Table 2 were more precise: 'Adam has a nice smile and lives five miles away … Justin is very close to his family and rides horses … Giovanni is heir to a palazzo in Venice … Christian travels the world surfing … Alex owns four properties in London.'

Miss Mae leant across to Leticia. 'I feel a bit bad that we're choosing the six bachelors to go through to dinner. Having said that, I have a lot of experience with men, and I know my chosen three will be perfect for the girls. Are you sure you won't let me put Paddy through as well?'

Leticia shook her head. 'Absolutely not! His hair is far too long, and he's listed his occupation as: "A bit of this and that". I've given in to you choosing a male model and someone with a very dubious name. I'm not giving in to that Irishman going through too. My chosen three have excellent backgrounds. You're lucky I've let you have any choice at all. I'm the experienced matchmaker around here.'

At the end of afternoon tea, the bachelors retired to the grand hallway, and the twins climbed the sweeping staircase to their rooms to change for dinner. Their clipboards were retrieved by Gerard, who raised his eyebrows at some of Tallulah's comments before handing them over to the Lady and Miss Mae.

Leticia spoke through gritted teeth. 'If I didn't know otherwise, I'd say that Tallulah is making a joke out of all of this and Tabitha is weak and indifferent. It is most appropriate that we won't be taking any of their opinions into account. I have inserted your chosen three bachelors with mine. See what you think of the final list.'

Miss Mae took the list from Leticia and read it out loud:

FOR TALLULAH

Alessandro – Greek shipping heir

Baron Pigstrotter of Pigstrotter Hall

George William – Remotely related to the Royal family

FOR TABITHA

Edward – Farmer

Felix – Doctor

Posterius – Male Model

To Leticia's dismay, Miss Mae tutted, before her eyes started to water. The Lady grabbed the list back and folded it neatly. 'I know they don't all make the criteria of inherited millionaires; I had to make the best of a bad bunch. Giovanni had been a front runner until you crossed him off due to his missing teeth. Teeth can be replaced unlike ancient palazzos in Venice.'

Miss Mae shook her head, then her shoulders joined force before she collapsed into a laughing heap on the floor, wiggling her ample posterior in the air.

'It's not that! Hahaha, oh my, oh my! There's no way Tallulah will move to Greece!'

Leticia tutted. 'Get up off the floor woman, and come with me into the grand hallway. We need to give the good news to the chosen six. The rest can make their way home.'

*

It was six-thirty before Mrs Carruthers and Arthur Makepeace saw any action. The arched doors of the chateau opened and a mixed bunch of bachelors came out either on their phones arranging transport, or laughing on their way down to the pub.

Paddy saluted to the couple in deckchairs and led the way for a group of unsuccessful bachelors. 'Follow me. I've been here before and I know of a nice little pub further down the High Street. I'm going to book in at the Solent Sea Guest House next door for a couple of nights – it's a shame to waste the weekend now that we've been "disqualified".'

7

THE CHOSEN ONES

A rustle from beneath the bedroom door made Tabitha jump. The make-up artist stopped applying eye shadow while Tabitha gathered up her turquoise satin and tulle evening dress and bent down to pick up the white envelope.

'Well, I guess this is it. Who have my fairy godmothers chosen as my top three?' Tabitha held the envelope to her chest and decided to wait to open it with Tallulah.

Tallulah was ready. She twirled around in her emerald satin, figure-hugging gown, with deep side split, and nearly toppled over on her silver stilettos when her envelope slid under the door. She opened it straight away. At first glance, she was disappointed that Paddy wasn't on the list. She'd been looking forward to continuing her Irish impersonation. She knew it hadn't fooled him, but it had been fun. What?? Not, the Piggy one! Nooooo way, was she going to become Lady of Pigstrotter Hall – she'd never even heard of it. The remote relative of the Royal family didn't appeal to her either. How remote? She couldn't even remember George William at the afternoon tea event. As far as Alessandro was concerned, she couldn't speak Greek. Nor did she want to learn to speak Greek. And to cap it all, she'd never been on a ship. Maybe one of Tabitha's "chosen few" would catch her eye.

Tallulah burst into Tabitha's room. 'I've got a Greek God, Mr Piggy and someone who is probably less related to the Royal family than us. Show me your list.'

Tabitha's stomach rolled with excitement as she opened her envelope. 'Let me see . . . I've got Edward, Felix and Posterius.'

'Who? I don't remember any of them. We've been well and truly stitched up.' Tallulah pulled the pins out of her piled-high hair and looked into the mirror as she scrunched it back into its natural shape.

Tabitha stood up and opened her evening bag before placing the names of her top three bachelors inside. 'If Lady Leticia is a bit naïve as far as men are concerned, then surely Miss Mae has had some experience? We shouldn't write the evening off yet. We may be surprised. I may find Mr Right between the farmer, doctor and model.'

Tallulah raised her eyes to the ceiling. Her sister was so gullible. Still, the doctor sounded all right and even the model. The farmer definitely wasn't her type though, Tabitha could have him. 'Come on, Tabitha, let's go and find our husbands!'

*

Two small tables were set at opposite ends of the candlelit dining room. Miss Mae clapped her hands excitedly. 'Oh, how I wish someone had done this for me as a young girl! Lady Leticia is a natural at this matchmaking business. There are now just two of you and six bachelors. You've each got a young man for starters, main course and dessert.'

Tallulah quipped: 'I was rather hoping for breaded prawns, spaghetti carbonara and sticky toffee pudding.' She looked around the room; the tables were so far apart. How would she be able to make eyes at Tabitha's doctor and model?

Lady Leticia knew the girl would be put in her place eventually. It was only a matter of time. Tabitha was the main worry; if she chose someone because she felt obliged to, then that would be a disaster. Leticia and Miss Mae needed to keep watch from afar to ensure that didn't happen.

Tallulah's first-course companion was Alessandro. He was very easy on the eye; the epitome of tall, dark and handsome *and* he spoke English fluently having been to Eton and Oxford University. There was no need for Tallulah to learn Greek. All in all, the first course went better than expected.

Tabitha wasn't enamoured with Edward who kept yawning and talking about the sheep shearing competition he'd won six years ago. He made it clear he wasn't a late-night person as he was always up at four in the morning to milk his cows. Tabitha didn't mind that, but it was only just after eight in the evening, and Edward was struggling to keep his eyes open.

The second-course bachelor could be defined as interesting for Tallulah. "Mr Piggy" somehow didn't fit the image of a Baron. He looked more like an Olympic rower; sandy, windswept hair, muscle-man physique. He also had a carefree attitude and good sense of humour. It was refreshing that he didn't talk about himself but asked about her, which she revelled in. She was recounting how disappointed she was to lose her treasured necklace when the second course finished. She'd been so enthralled with elaborating on her life that she hadn't had time to even glance over at Tabitha's doctor.

Felix, the doctor, was nice enough and pleasant to look at but Tabitha didn't warm to his detailed account of ingrowing toenails and his analysis that prevention was far better than cure as it would save millions of pounds for the NHS.

At the third course, Tallulah was pleasantly surprised by George William. She didn't get a chance to ask him how closely he was related to the Royal family as he wanted to know all about her; from her time at school to when she studied at art school in London with Tabitha. George William didn't look very Royal with his buzzcut hairstyle and nearly black eyes; Tallulah thought he looked more suited to the Royal Marines than the Royal family.

Tabitha was left sitting alone, staring at two plates of Limoncello tart, a jug of cream and a plate of frangipane biscotti. Where was Posterius? Lady Leticia and Miss Mae were propped up at the bar in the corner of the room with a bottle of sherry and four of the remaining bachelors. Tabitha looked over at Tallulah who was obviously enjoying talking about herself to George William, and she suddenly felt very alone. Even Gerard had given up keeping an eye on proceedings and was probably in the kitchen eating his well-earned dinner. There was only one thing for it. Tabitha had to find Posterius.

The information on the Reception Desk was easy to follow. Six rooms had been allocated for the successful bachelors. Tabitha climbed the stairs and knocked on each one. There was no answer. So, she knocked on each one again, this time announcing herself loudly. 'Posterius, this is Tabitha, how dare you stand me up? You are the lowest of the low and should be ashamed of yourself. You may be a model, but your name sounds like a back....'

The door in front of Tabitha opened, and a strong, tanned arm reached out to grab her, pulling her into the bedroom. A large hand covered her mouth to suppress her scream. 'Don't be alarmed, Tabitha, I'm Posterius.'

8

EVERYONE DOWN TO
THE KING ARTHUR

In the King Arthur public house, the atmosphere was buzzing. Matilda and Cindy were on a girls' night out, with Theo and Jamie minding the little ones back at Villa Tressler and Villa Summer and Clive and Arthur were ensconced at a table next to the window. Arthur twisted his silver moustache. 'I've got a bad feeling, Clive. The twins don't have a hope of finding boyfriends amongst any of that lot Leticia's found for them.'

Clive's turquoise eyes twinkled. 'I still can't believe you sat outside Chateau Amore de Pebblio all afternoon in a deckchair with Mrs Carruthers!'

'Two deckchairs, Clive, two deckchairs.'

'I know, Arthur. But those girls need a bit of space to find the loves of their lives. Did I ever tell you about my past lady friends?'

'Only that your villas are named after three of them: Julianna, Elena and Veronique. That's all I need to know, Clive. Too much detail would be intruding.'

Clive sighed. 'I met Veronique in Paris; she was special.'

Arthur stared at his friend. 'If she was good enough to have a villa named after her, why didn't you put a ring on her finger?'

'It wasn't that simple.'

'Strikes me, she got lucky if you had the other two on the go at the same time.'

'Oh no, Julianna was my first love when I was very young. I regrettably left Elena for Jamie's mother, who was nothing but a scam artist. She was one of the biggest mistakes of my life. It doesn't pay to be privileged, so to speak. There is no-one out there you can trust.'

'You can trust me.'

'I know that, Arthur. I am thankful for that every day.'

Arthur nodded towards the bar. 'You see that lot chatting up Matilda and Cindy? Well, they're the dropouts from this afternoon's matchmaking session at the castle.'

'Well, let's keep an eye on things then, Arthur. A few spurned bachelors talking to Cindy and Matilda doesn't make for a good recipe. If nothing else, I can be the eyes and ears for Jamie.'

'Another pint, Clive? I'll just pop up to the bar and get them in. I'll listen out for any untoward discussions while I'm up there.'

Paddy was keen to speak to Matilda. 'So, Tabitha and Tallulah are your sisters. Have they travelled much? Seen the world?'

Matilda sipped her prosecco and chose her words carefully before answering. 'The furthest the twins have been is London – they went to art school there. Come to think of it; I've never really thought about it before.'

Cindy chipped in. 'Not like their sisters, eh? Matilda's worked in New York and Hannah in Dubai. I've not even been to London, so I can't talk. I've lived here all my life; Truelove Hills has given me everything I need.'

Arthur carried the pints back to Clive. 'Nothing to worry about there. The men are only interested in Tabitha and Tallulah; they're just draining Matilda and Cindy of information.'

By ten o'clock, the bachelors had dispersed, with the exception of Paddy. Matilda and Cindy had been enjoying his company. They were surprised he'd been disqualified as they were sure the twins would have loved him; he was keen to know everything about them. There was no doubt he'd kissed the Blarney Stone at some point. Cindy looked at her watch. 'Well, that's us for tonight. We'd best be off, or our husbands won't let us loose again if we miss our curfew.'

Paddy waved as the girls left the pub. Matilda held the door open for two young men to enter then reached for her phone. 'We should have taken a photo of Paddy to show the twins. Let's take a quick one through the window. Look, he's not looking, he's chatting to those two men that just went in. He'd chat to anyone that one, I really enjoyed his company tonight.'

Bruce Copperfield was behind the bar. He was pleased that his sister, Cindy, had finally gone home. She had been having too much fun with that Irishman for his liking and, as for the matchmaking event at the chateau, well, that was a waste of time. He was the one for Tallulah. He'd only taken on a new girlfriend to make her jealous; she just needed a wake-up call after dumping him for no good reason.

Arthur and Clive were struggling to concentrate on their game of dominoes. Paddy was now huddled together with those two men that had just entered the pub.

'Keep your voice down, Ryan. Everyone knows

everyone in this pub. That's good for intelligence but not good if we blow our cover. Why are you and Pete here anyway? Where's Nick?'

'That's just the point, Sir. Nick's gone missing. He didn't turn up for dessert and Tabitha went after him. Pete managed to keep Tallulah's attention, and she didn't even notice. Mind you, she drank three glasses of wine with her main course and kept calling me "Mr Piggy", which I didn't find amusing.'

Paddy's eyes twinkled. 'We need to have a bit of fun in our line of business. It was very good of you to take on the title Baron Pigstrotter; I can't believe they fell for it. Pete got off lightly with George William.' Paddy checked his phone. 'Nick hasn't been in contact; I suggest you both get back to the chateau and keep your ears to the ground. Cover for him if he doesn't turn up soon.'

*

Back at the chateau, Tallulah was convinced that the matchmaking weekend wasn't going to be such a disaster after all. She'd enjoyed the meals with Alessandro, Baron Pigstrotter and George William.

After searching the cloakroom, and Tabitha's bedroom, she came to the conclusion that her sister's evening had gone even better with the farmer, doctor and male model. Crafty Tabitha. If Lady Leticia and Miss Mae found out that she had disappeared with one of the bachelors, then all hell would break loose. The best thing was to get an early night and say that Tabitha had done the same.

By the time Ryan and Pete arrived back at the chateau, Alessandro and Felix were still at the bar, and Edward had retired early. There was no sign of Nick (aka Posterius) or either of the twins.

Ryan's phone vibrated with a text message from Paddy:

NICK'S TAKEN TABITHA TO THE SAFE PLACE.

PROTECT TALLULAH.

Ryan showed the message to Pete, who nodded before heading outside and scaling the chateau walls to reach Tallulah's open bedroom window. Ryan sent a text to Paddy:

PLAN V IN OPERATION.

9

A CHANGE OF PLAN

At breakfast the next morning, there were six bachelors but no sign of the twins. Gerard had knocked on their bedroom doors at the request of Lady Leticia, but there was no answer.

Leticia paced around the grand hallway. Miss Mae tried to calm her down. 'Don't worry; there must be a good explanation.' Miss Mae's phone rang, and she stepped outside to answer it.

When she returned, her face was calm, compared to the ruddiness creeping up Lady Leticia's neck and cheeks. 'That was Tallulah. The twins both send their thanks for everything we've done but, in their heart of hearts, they don't believe that love is on the horizon this weekend. They've decided to take themselves away for a while for a bit of a break.'

The Lady stopped pacing and stamped her foot. 'Those girls are incorrigible! What will we tell the remaining bachelors?'

Miss Mae shrugged her shoulders. 'Just tell them the truth, that none of them is any good and that the girls have gone in search of love elsewhere.'

*

Lady Leticia stood in the courtyard of the chateau, next to the replica Trevi Fountain, handing out leaflets to the departing bachelors. 'I had high hopes for you, Baron Pigstrotter, and you, George William. You were both very engaging with Tallulah. Alessandro is the richest and best looking, of course, but you did yourselves proud. Please take a leaflet with the dates of my future matchmaking events. There'll be more girls to choose from next time.'

Once outside, and on the High Street, Ryan elbowed Pete and winked at a waiting Nick. 'We should be proud we got through to the final six, we all beat our boss! Paddy will be gutted he got disqualified so early on. It'll be the long hair that did it; the Lady wouldn't be impressed with that.'

Nick laughed and held his phone aloft. 'Another day of being called "Posterius" would have sent me round the bend. Read this message from Paddy; it's just come through.'

MISSION DELAYED. DISPERSE.

Ryan winked. 'That's "Paddy Code" for: *Don't go too far. Act normally. Next major panic around the corner. And, above all, be there when I need you.*'

Pete laughed. 'That about sums it up.'

Ryan turned to face Nick. 'What really happened last night. Why did you stand Tabitha up for dessert?'

Nick's cheeks flushed, and he pushed his fists into his trouser pockets before hanging his head. 'I swear there was a guy stalking Tabitha in the chateau. He kept popping up from nowhere and staring at her. It wasn't natural. Anyway, I decided to follow him during the main course. He was walking through the grounds of the chateau towards the sea. I was taking cover behind a tree when I felt a warm, wet sensation on my leg and heard a maid screaming: "Fluffy, I knew I shouldn't have let you in".'

Ryan and Pete couldn't contain their fits of laughter.

Nick raised his hands in the air. 'OK, so I got peed on by a dog. I ran up to my room to take a quick shower and missed dessert. I didn't expect Tabitha to come looking for me. I was still concerned about the stalker, so I took her to the safe place. Paddy wasn't happy about it when I told him. The twins are now in the safe place too early, and my punishment is to make sure they don't do a runner.'

Pete wiped tears of laughter from his eyes. 'How are you going to do that?'

'Well, I'm supposed to be a male model, remember? I'll go jogging up and down the beach in full view of Villa Veronique.'

Ryan grinned. 'With your shirt off, of course.'

'Of course.'

Pete reached for his wallet. 'Well, I'll help out. You go and flex your muscles, and I'll impress the girls with my cooking skills. We can't have them going hungry now, can we?'

Ryan slapped Nick on the back and high-fived Pete. 'Sounds like you two have it sorted. I'd best be off. Too many bachelors hanging around the village will cause suspicion. Look after those girls now and don't do anything I wouldn't do, particularly with the vivacious Tallulah.'

*

David Makepeace was sure he hadn't heard the telephone ring in the guest house. Still, he was grateful that Paddy had answered it and taken the message from Tallulah. Paddy advised David that the twins had given up on the matchmaking weekend and were taking a short holiday instead. Paddy hadn't asked how long they'd be away. David scratched his head. They were booked in for shifts at the pub next week, and it wasn't like them just to take off. His daughters could be difficult at times, well at least Tallulah could. She was most likely annoyed that Lady Leticia and Miss Mae were trying to get them married off and had disappeared with Tabitha by way of a protest. Those girls were best left alone with no-one interfering. On top of that, Paddy had cut short his two-night stay at the guest house and had left after breakfast. Lost revenue and now temporary staff to sort out. It had been a bad start to the day.

*

At Sonning Hall, Clive searched through a box of old photographs. He'd found one of Julianna, a few of Elena and right down at the bottom – there it was – a photograph of him kissing Veronique at the top of the Eiffel Tower. If her husband had ever found out, they wouldn't have shared the magical two weeks in Paris that spring. Poor Veronique, trapped in a loveless marriage to a gangland boss. There was never going to be a way out for her. Clive had commissioned a bespoke necklace with an Eiffel Tower charm for Veronique. It was encrusted with diamonds, and their initials were discretely engraved underneath the tower. He'd managed to have it delivered to her, and she had worn it. He'd seen her wearing it in the society newspapers prior to her death the year after they parted.

*

Matilda popped in to see Cindy at the bakery. 'Can you believe it! The matchmaking weekend's been aborted, and the twins have run off to take some time away for themselves. I've just seen Miss Mae in the Post Office & General Store. Mrs Carruthers is aghast. Apparently, she'd been taking bets on which of the twins would get married first, and now she's got to hand all the money back. Miss Mae's consoling her. Those two are like chalk and cheese, but they get on so well. It's nice for Mrs Carruthers to have a friend.'

The door to the bakery opened, and Hannah strode in. Cindy rushed around the counter and pulled out a chair for her at one of the small tables. Hannah smiled. 'Stop fussing over me, I'm only pregnant and feeling much better now, I might add. Anyway, I'm sure you've heard the news. Gossip spreads like wildfire in this village. Will Tomlin was in work this morning at the vineyard, and he gave Toby and me the lowdown on the matchmaking event. If anyone had asked me, then I would have told them the event was a non-starter.'

Cindy brought a tray of tea and scones over, and the three women sat together, undertaking a post-mortem of events at the chateau. Matilda was intrigued.

'Ooooh, this is exciting! What inside info did Will get? Did he see everything going on? How is he getting on living in your old house, Hannah? I bet Lady Leticia treats him like a long-lost son, living in the grounds of the chateau. Go on, what did he say?'

Hannah sipped her tea. 'Well, he said the whole thing was laughable. He didn't have any plans on Saturday night, so he mingled with the bachelors in the chateau bar at one point. It sounds like they were taking turns to eat dinner with the twins. Apparently, they had a bachelor for each course. Anyway, one of them who was called Posterius was particularly shady.'

Cindy snorted. 'Posterius! What sort of a name is that?'

Hannah continued, 'He's a male model, so that explains the name. He's just trying to draw attention to himself to get more bookings from agencies. No-one would forget a name like that. Anyway, Will said that Posterius acted like he was in a James Bond movie. He was stalking the place, peering around corners, running up the stairs two at a time, hiding behind trees, generally acting weirdly. Will said that, at one point, he thought Posterius was reaching inside his jacket to produce a gun. How silly is that?'

Matilda's eyes widened. 'Do you know who Posterius was having dinner with? Was it Tallulah or Tabitha?'

Hannah looked over her shoulder then leant forward onto the table before lowering her voice. 'Well, we need to make sure that Lady Leticia and Miss Mae don't find out, but Will saw Posterius running up the stairs shortly before Tabitha disappeared up them. Will said that neither of them ate their dessert and that their chaperones were too tipsy to notice. He'd never seen Leticia drink so much sherry; he's sure Miss Mae's a bad influence on her.'

Cindy sat back and wiped her hands on her apron. 'So, it sounds like the weekend wasn't a complete disaster, Tabitha was keen on Posterius. Good for her to let her hair down, she's only young once.'

Hannah rubbed her small bump. 'Oh, to be young again. If I'm this big now, then what am I going to be like by February? Anyway, the real reason I popped in was to invite you all to the vineyard for a post-wedding party. Toby's insisting that we do something now I'm feeling better. How does two weeks today sound?'

Matilda clapped her hands. 'That's wonderful! I love a good party. It'll make up for us not being Maids of Honour. What do you think, Cindy? We could wear long dresses and put flowers in our hair, that will help us feel less deprived about missing my eldest sister's wedding to the most eligible bachelor in the area; Mr Tobias Finchinglake, vineyard owner and emerald heir.'

Cindy laughed. 'Well, we'll certainly pull out all the stops to help make it a good do! Count us in, Hannah. Jamie will be keen to sample Finchinglake's latest wines.'

Hannah went to stand up, and Matilda grabbed her hand. 'Where do you think you're going? We need to choose an outfit for you. We can search online over another cup of tea.'

10

TIME TO MOVE ON

Mrs Carruthers was grateful for Miss Mae's help in clearing out the loft of the Post Office & General Store. Miss Mae had scaled the ladder several times this morning and was hardly out of breath.

'May I question why you are having such a big clear out, Mrs Carruthers? It's nearer to autumn than spring. Most of us have a surge of energy earlier on in the year to undertake the jobs we're not always partial to do at other times.'

Mrs Carruthers ripped the brown tape off yet another box. 'I've been on a constant clear-out for over a year now. My accommodation next to the shop was the starting point as that contains my family heirlooms.

I normally keep anything important in there. The loft in the shop has been a sticking point for me as, with my knees, I wasn't relishing the thought of popping in and out of that loft hatch.'

Miss Mae sat on the boarded floor of the loft and contemplated the reasoning behind Mrs Carruthers' actions. She had heard from members of the community that Mrs Carruthers would never retire – she was well into her seventies and still very sprightly. The shop was her life.

'Are you all right up there? It's gone very quiet. I'm waiting for the next box.'

'I'm fine, Mrs Carruthers, I'm just assessing the remaining stock up here, only fifteen more boxes to go.'

Less than an hour later, Miss Mae closed the loft hatch before sliding down the ladder. 'Yippee! Not done that since I was a girl. Those rungs just get in the way. It's all about a loose grip and nerves of steel.'

Mrs Carruthers stood open-mouthed. That woman was bionic; she was sure of it. There had never been anyone like her in Truelove Hills before.

*

Clive couldn't get Veronique out of his head. He strolled around the grounds of Sonning Hall, racking his brains. The last time he'd spoken to her, she told him that she didn't have long left and that she would write to him. He never received a letter. If he had received a letter, he would have something from her to keep. He was a just an old romantic naming a villa after Veronique; he knew that. It was his way of having something in memory of his long-lost love. He had the photograph of them both, but somehow that wasn't enough.

Clive hadn't set foot inside Villa Veronique since it had been finished and fully furnished in Parisienne style. He checked the booking schedule for his three villas that Theo kept updated online. Villa Veronique wasn't booked out this week. Maybe the only way to escape his demons was to meet them head-on. Clive checked Tristan's diary. Jamie wasn't using him over the next couple of days. Clive picked up his phone. 'Take me to Truelove Hills, Tristan. I have a feeling in my bones that I should visit Villa Veronique. I have left it far too long to escape my past. It's time to move on.'

*

Miss Mae felt rejuvenated following her morning in the shop. She skipped down the High Street, waving at the occasional chuckling tourist and was just opening the door to Villa Elena when Clive's Bentley purred up the pebblestone lane and stopped outside Villa Veronique. Miss Mae rushed to greet him.

'Clive! How lovely to see you in these parts. You must come with me now and have some brunch, lunch, even dinner!'

Miss Mae linked arms with Clive and dragged him into Villa Elena. He marvelled at the strength of the woman. He'd always thought Miss Mae was a bit eccentric, but she was surpassing herself now. If he didn't know better, he sensed she was quite nervous on this occasion.

'Now, Clive, I'd like to thank you for letting Villa Elena to me long-term.'

'The pleasure's all mine, Miss Mae, all mine. I must admit though that it would surely be cheaper for you to rent elsewhere in the village if you are aiming to remain here for some time. I understand you are managing the nursery and have become quite a popular figure in the community.'

Miss Mae nodded, and Clive sensed she was distracted. 'I'll just pop into the kitchen to make our dinner. Will sausage and chips do?'

Clive stood up. 'There's really no need Miss Mae. Really no need at all.'

Miss Mae peered around the kitchen door. 'Oh, yes there is, Clive. Yes, there is. You take a seat, and I'll be done in a jiffy.' The kitchen door slammed, and Clive sat down as instructed.

TRUELOVE HILLS – THE MATCHMAKER

*

It was the next to last box, and Mrs Carruthers had found it. It had pricked her conscience for years, but without being able to find it, she couldn't do anything about it.

Many years ago, a small package had been delivered to the Post Office. It was addressed to: '*Lord Clive, South England.*'

Mrs Carruthers knew everyone and everyone in the Post Office Services knew her. They didn't know how to deliver the package so they entrusted it with Mrs Carruthers who said she would find a way to ensure it got to its destination.

It wasn't Mrs Carruthers' fault. She didn't know that Lord Sonning-Smythe of Sonning Hall was called "Clive" by his friends, she only found that out two years ago when he funded the development of Truelove Hills.

With no sign of a Lord Clive in the South of England at the time, Mrs Carruthers put the package in her "undelivered items" sack. Several years later, Mrs Carruthers opened all the undelivered items and placed any saleable objects on the donations table for a charity auction. She threw away any perishables and was pleased that the Post Office & General Store smelt a lot better after her clear out.

The package addressed to '*Lord Clive, South England*' was the most intriguing one. It contained an Eiffel Tower necklace and a note:

Mon Chéri Clive,

You are my greatest love.

V x

*

Paddy and Ryan were eating lunch in a pub in the next village when Paddy received a text.

ABORT PLAN V. ABORT.

Nick was jogging along the beach in front of Villa Veronique, and Pete was in Cindy's delicatessen buying provisions when they both received the same message:

ABORT PLAN V. REGROUP. ACTION PLAN P.

11

CODE 'P' FOR PARIS

Tallulah and Tabitha were having the time of their lives. Firstly, they'd been "kidnapped" by Posterius and George William (who had since admitted they were called Nick and Pete and had given themselves fake names as a bit of a joke at the matchmaking event) and had spent last night in Villa Veronique. It was all so exciting; the matchmaking weekend had turned out much better than expected. The bachelors were full of surprises.

Tabitha was watching Nick running along the beach before he stopped abruptly and took an about-turn. He was now heading to the villa. The twins could quite see how Nick was a male model. He was tall, tanned with messy dark brown hair and steel blue eyes. They could just imagine him strutting his stuff down the catwalk during London or Paris fashion week.

Pete ran into the villa before Nick. 'Come on girls; we're off on an adventure. There's a private plane waiting for us; we're off to Paris!'

The twins grabbed their bags and watched as the boys smoothed the cushions on the sofa, straightened the beds and wiped the kitchen free of all activity, including grabbing the bin bag. Tallulah was amazed at the speed and dexterity with which they worked.

The girls were ushered out of the villa within minutes and into a blacked-out car. Tallulah shrieked when she saw the driver. 'Not Mr Piggy! Please tell me *you* have another name too.'

A smiling Mr Piggy turned around. 'You can call me Ryan.'

Nick jumped into the front seat, and Pete joined the twins in the back. This was all too exciting to ask questions, but something was bothering Tabitha. 'We don't have passports.'

Ryan looked at the girls in his rear-view mirror. 'No need to worry about that, Paddy's got everything sorted, and he's meeting us at the airport.'

Tallulah's heart leapt. 'Paddy's still around? Don't tell me that's not his real name either?'

Pete chuckled. 'Paddy will always be Paddy; we'd never call him anything else.'

Tabitha frowned. 'It sounds like you all know each other. Had you met before this weekend?'

Ryan glanced sideways at Nick, and Pete answered on their behalf. 'We all used to work together. You know what it's like. Never lose touch that sort of thing.'

Nick cringed in advance of Tallulah's questioning. 'So, let me see, Nick's a male model, Pete's related to the Royal family and Ryan's Baron Pigstrotter of Pigstrotter Hall. You're all having a laugh, aren't you? We're not off to Paris, are we? Please tell me we're not being abducted. Our father isn't rich; he owns a guest house and a pub. *We're* not rich either; we work as his slaves.'

Ryan's eyes twinkled, that girl had attitude, there were no flies on her. 'You're right, we're all action men working for an elite special forces team, and we're abducting you to have the time of your lives. Two attractive girls like you deserve a bit of fun. Are you up for it?'

Tabitha giggled. 'I'm up for it! What about you, Tallulah?'

Tallulah narrowed her eyes. 'What's Paddy's job?'

Ryan sensed he had competition with Paddy for Tallulah's affection. Still, he liked a challenge. 'Oh, Paddy's someone we use to help us out sometimes. He didn't make the grade in the fitness stakes. Or, in the matchmaking ones either.'

*

Clive managed to escape Miss Mae's offer of sausages and chips. She said the sausages had burned and the chips were soggy. She explained it wasn't possible to be good at everything before pushing Clive towards her front door and waving him off.

Clive shook his head; he had never met anyone quite like her before. He felt grateful that she wasn't a good cook at least he could now get on with what he'd come to do, and he unlocked the door to Villa Veronique.

*

Paddy helped Tallulah out of the car. 'To be sure, I wasn't planning meeting up with this fair maiden again any time soon.'

Tallulah huffed. 'You worked out that I'm not really Irish, didn't you?'

Paddy widened his bright blue eyes which were framed to perfection by long black eyelashes. 'Irish? Now, wherever would I get that idea from? Red hair, green eyes and a shamrock necklace? Now they may have been clues, but as soon as you spoke, I could tell you were English through and through.'

Tallulah folded her arms and tapped her foot.

Paddy ignored her and leant in the car to help Tabitha out. 'Now, come along everyone, there's a plane to catch.'

*

Clive didn't want to stay in the villa for long; he didn't need to. He didn't know why he had left it for so many years to say his goodbyes. The villa was just a house; it wasn't a person. OK, he'd given it her name, but Veronique was long gone, and he was just a silly old fool.

There were roses in the garden, and Clive picked a white one before making his way down to the beach. The tide was going out, and as he threw the rose into the sea, he whispered, 'Goodbye Veronique.'

A cough came from behind, and Clive turned around. Mrs Carruthers was standing a few feet away. Had she heard him? She'd definitely seen him. Mrs Carruthers held out a sealed envelope. 'This is for you, Clive. It arrived years ago with a necklace, but I didn't know you were called Clive at the time. I didn't know anyone called Clive. Goodness knows how long it had been in the postal system. All wasn't lost as the necklace went to charity; Tallulah bought it with her first wages at the Post Office & General Store. How nice was that? Very fitting, don't you think? Anyway, I must be off now. Take the letter; I didn't read it.'

Mrs Carruthers walked back up the beach, and Clive ripped open the envelope and read the note:

Mon Chéri Clive,

You are my greatest love.

V x

Veronique hadn't forgotten him. She'd written as promised, and she'd tried to return the necklace to him before she died. Clive spun around and watched the white rose bobbing on the ocean. He pressed the paper to his lips, then folded it neatly before placing it back inside the envelope. This was a sign. It was all he needed. It was time to move on.

12

A JOB TO DO

Paddy ensured the twins and his team were safely on board the private jet before making his exit.

Tallulah shouted after him. 'I thought you were coming with us.'

Paddy turned around before climbing down the aircraft steps. 'I've got a job to do here. It's not easy being the boss. Enjoy Paris.' Tallulah scowled at Ryan who pretended not to notice.

Paddy received another text message.

ALL CLEAR.

When Paddy reached Villa Elena, Miss Mae opened the door. 'That was a close one, Paddy. Clive's not shown any interest in visiting Villa Veronique until now. I can't believe we've had the twins under surveillance for months and that G1 decides to come to the UK the weekend of the matchmaking event.'

Paddy looked over his shoulder before entering the villa. 'What's the latest intelligence on G1?'

Miss Mae tapped away on a computer. 'He's within a five-mile radius of Truelove Hills.'

Paddy grinned. 'Time for a pint at the pub then. Are you up for it?'

Miss Mae grabbed her bag. 'I'm always up for it!'

*

Bruce Copperfield pulled the pints. With the twins away on their unscheduled break, David Makepeace had cancelled all leave for Bruce and his brother Steve. Bruce was moodier than ever and spoke loudly to his brother. 'So, what's the reason a stray bachelor has turned up again around here? The twins have run as far away as possible from the bunch of losers that turned up at the weekend.'

Miss Mae tutted. 'Very rude.'

Paddy turned around to face Bruce. 'Would you like to take this outside?'

Bruce reached for a tea towel and started polishing

glasses. 'I didn't mean to cause offence. I just make a point of watching out for the twins. Steve and I went to school with them, and they're like sisters to us.'

Paddy sipped his pint. 'Is that so? I'll keep a mental note of that.'

Miss Mae gestured for Paddy to join her at a table next to the window. 'Those Copperfield brothers are harmless. I'm told that Bruce courted Tallulah for a while and Tabitha spurned Steve's advances. There's nothing more sinister than that.'

Paddy watched the brothers trying not to watch him. He winked at Miss Mae. 'They may come in useful. We could use them as decoys.'

Miss Mae raised her eyebrows. 'Won't that be dangerous?'

Paddy stood up and headed to the bar. 'Not if they do as they're told.'

Paddy placed his empty glass on the bar and took a photograph out of his pocket. He signalled to Bruce and Steve to join him. 'Would you be up for helping a poor old bachelor out?'

Bruce scoffed. 'What's in it for us?'

Paddy held up the photograph. 'Nothing, except saving this guy a huge amount of embarrassment. He's a missing bachelor. He didn't turn up this weekend because the other fellas thought he was the favourite for Tallulah.'

Bruce scrutinised the photograph. 'What happened to him?'

Paddy put the photograph back in his pocket. 'Well now, that would be telling. If you were tied naked to the railings at Buckingham Palace, would you want people knowing?' Bruce and Steve's eyes widened, and Paddy continued, 'No, I thought not. I've been informed that he's making his way here now to win Tallulah's hand in marriage. He's heard the matchmaking weekend was a disaster, but he doesn't know the twins have gone on a little holiday. If you see him, please call me. Here's my card.'

Bruce took the card from Paddy. 'It just says "Paddy" with a phone number.'

Paddy touched his nose. 'To be sure, that's all you need to know. You wouldn't want Tallulah running off with some eejit who's exposed himself in London, would you? I'm the best man to sort this out.'

Miss Mae rushed to the door and pulled Paddy behind her before whispering. 'You certainly have a good imagination. I'll give you that! We'll go back to mine and lie low until the morning.'

Paddy grinned. 'Why, Miss Mae! If I didn't know better, I could be led to believe you are propositioning me.'

Miss Mae did a twirl and patted her hair. 'Never judge a book by its cover!'

*

It was late when the group arrived in Paris. Nick checked in at the hotel reception and came away with three keys. 'We've hit the jackpot, three rooms next to each other. Hopefully, you girls are OK with sharing. Ryan and Pete will take the room on the right of yours, and I'll take the left. They've all got balconies with views of the Eiffel Tower. Let's go up and make the most of what's left of the evening. I've ordered drinks and supper to be sent to our rooms. Meet you outside on the balconies in ten minutes.'

Nick helped the twins into their room then joined Ryan and Pete in theirs. 'The latest intelligence is that G1 is staying overnight five-miles from Truelove Hills. There's a good chance he's planning the abduction for tomorrow. We have a very small window before he discovers the twins are missing. Paris is a safe place until tomorrow lunchtime. Paddy says we shouldn't stay here later than that. When G1 realises the girls aren't in England, he'll get his Paris associates on the case, and we won't stand a chance.'

13

WHEN PLANS GO WRONG

Paris was magical, and the hotel so close to the Eiffel Tower was fantastic. The twins had been tired the previous evening and didn't complain too much when Nick suggested they were all in bed by eleven. The worst thing was that it had been a balmy night and he insisted they all closed and locked their balcony doors. Nick was turning out to be a real worrier. Anyway, it was morning now, and the girls were keen to enjoy their adventure.

Morning coffee and croissants at a café on the Champs-Élysées was rushed because the twins insisted on visiting the Eiffel Tower. Nick kept looking at his watch. 'We have to go now if you want to see the tower. Our deadline is lunchtime.'

Nick was such a bore. Tallulah rolled her eyes, and

Tabitha huffed. Why bring them to Paris and not let them visit the attractions? Come to think of it, Ryan and Pete were edgy this morning. Tallulah suspected they'd hit the minibar after their eleven o'clock curfew. She wished she'd done the same.

As they tried to keep up with Nick's pace down the Champ de Mars, someone caught Tabitha's eye. 'Isn't that Clive over there?' A quick-thinking Tallulah pushed Tabitha sideways into the crowd.

'Clive! Clive! It's us, what are you doing here?'

Clive was stunned. 'Oh, hello, Tallulah. Tabitha. I could ask you the same thing.'

Tallulah watched the frantic bachelors searching for them and steered Clive and Tabitha in the opposite direction. 'How long are you here for, Clive?'

'Oh, I'm just on a flying visit so to speak. I needed to put some memories to rest at the Eiffel Tower, and now Tristan is going to fly me home.'

Tallulah grabbed Clive's arm. 'Can we come with you, pleeeease? Some of the bachelors have abducted us. They've got money to waste bringing us here, but they've turned out to be boring and dull. It's more fun working in the pub than living a jet-setting life.'

Clive patted her hand and smiled; he was accustomed to Tallulah's tendency to over-exaggerate.

In fact, he quite enjoyed her exuberant style. 'The trouble is, you young ladies haven't found the right gentlemen yet. There's lots of time to do that. No need to rush. Do you need to let your young men know that I'm giving you a lift home?'

Tabitha took hold of Clive's other arm. 'There's no need. Let them sweat. We didn't get a say in whether we wanted to come here. Lady Leticia and Miss Mae will be so disappointed that the matchmaking weekend was a disaster. We shouldn't have let those fakes sweep us off our feet, so to speak.'

*

Paddy's phone rang. It was Nick. 'We're at the foot of the Eiffel Tower, and the twins have gone missing. They were desperate to come here, so the only conclusion we can come to is that G1's associates have intercepted them.'

*

At the airport, Tallulah stopped outside a jewellery shop. 'I used to have an Eiffel Tower necklace like that one. Only mine was prettier.'

Clive rubbed his forehead. 'Where is the necklace now, Tallulah?'

'I don't know. I last wore it for the gig race. There's a good chance it's at the bottom of the ocean after Lady Leticia's speedboat nearly drowned us all. It's so annoying as I wore it whenever I needed good luck. I'm sure it helped me pass my art exams in London. It certainly caused a bit of a stir back then.'

Clive was intrigued. 'Why did the necklace cause a stir?'

'A French student took a special interest in it. He took photographs of me wearing it and said he would give them to his father when the time was right. Whatever that meant.'

Clive closed his eyes; he knew the answer to his next question. 'What was the name of the French student?'

'Francois Garibaldi the second. Rumour had it that his father, the first Francois Garibaldi, was a gangster.'

Clive shuddered. He had a bad feeling about all of this. Paris wasn't a good place to be with the Garibaldi's still around; it was much safer in Truelove Hills. He held onto the twins' arms tightly. 'Come along, young ladies. Let's get you home.'

*

The flight back to England gave the girls time to take stock. What a whirlwind couple of days! Four of the bachelors pretending to be part of a crack team to attract their attention. What was that all about? Still, all of them had been easy on the eye, if not relaxed in their nature.

Now the twins didn't know what to think, or who to believe. Nick, Ryan and Pete were self-confessed tricksters. But why? Still, Paddy was Paddy; he'd been Paddy all along, as wild and Irish as they went. He was the only genuine one, but why was he involved with the others and pretending to be their boss? Nothing added up. Nothing.

There was only one thing for it, the girls needed to get their own back on a group of losers who had deliberately fooled them, and a spoiled their weekend.

14

IN HIDING

Clive's Bentley stopped outside the King Arthur public house, and the twins jumped out. Clive climbed out too. 'Are you going inside to let your father know you are home?'

Tallulah grabbed Tabitha by the arm. 'We're just popping over to see Matilda first in her shop to let her know we're back.'

Clive waved. 'Good idea, I'll pop into your Grandfather's and ask him to join me in the pub for a pint, it's a bit early at four o'clock, but I don't expect Arthur will mind. I'll let him know I found you both in Paris, or rather you found me, if that's acceptable?'

The twins were already on the other side of the

road, and Tallulah waved back. 'That's great, Clive. Thanks for the lift!'

When Clive was inside Arthur's cottage, Tallulah dragged Tabitha down the pebblestone lane leading to the Sea View Villas. Tabitha winced. 'Let go of my arm, where are you taking me?'

'We're going into hiding for a few hours to teach the boys a lesson. Word will soon get around that Clive brought us home, and that would be far too easy a solution for those pranksters. It isn't on that they had a laugh at our expense. Trust me; they need to stew for a while. They'll think we got abducted behind Clive's back when we were dropped off at the pub.'

'But won't Daddy and Grandpa be worried?'

'No chance. They know what we're like; up to no good as usual. It's only the bachelors that will be worried. Just a few hours should do it.'

Tallulah knocked on the door of Villa Elena, and Miss Mae opened it. 'It's the twins!!'

Tallulah smiled her best smile. 'Yes, it's us, Miss Mae. We know that the nursery is shut today, with it being a Bank Holiday and all that and we know that you will be upset that we're not betrothed by now as the matchmaking event ended early. Well, you need to know that none of that is your fault. There was a rogue group of bachelors who fancied themselves as some sort of special services hitmen. Nick, you'll know him as Posterius, abducted Tabitha first, then George William – whose real name is Pete – scaled the wall of the chateau and carried me out of my bedroom window. Don't tell Clive, but we both stayed in Villa Veronique overnight, before three of the bachelors took us to Paris. That Pigstrotter bloke is really called Ryan, and he turned up in a blacked-out car to drive us to the airport. It was hardly worth going as we were only there for a night. They were keen to leave Paris this morning. We didn't even get to see the Eiffel Tower properly.'

Miss Mae looked both ways down the pebblestone lane, pulled the twins inside the villa, and shut the door. 'Oh, my goodness! At least you're safe now. How did you get home?'

It was Tabitha's turn to speak. 'Well, you'll never believe it, but we bumped into Clive, and he gave us a lift home. Private jet, Bentley, the works! I must admit I feel bad going along with Tallulah's idea to go into hiding for a few hours so that the bachelors get worried about us. Tallulah wants them to learn a lesson for ruining our weekend. To be honest, she was gutted that Paddy didn't make it through the first round, she's got a soft spot for him, although she'll never admit it.'

The sound of broken glass in the kitchen made Miss Mae jump and the girls scream. Miss Mae rushed to the kitchen door. 'Nothing to worry about, it'll be my pet . . . my pet seagull. Yes, that's it! I'll need to shut the window. I really shouldn't encourage it. Messy old thing.'

Miss Mae returned to the lounge and drew the curtains. 'It's very sunny today; I don't want the furniture fading. You girls make yourselves at home by taking a seat on the sofa. This is a lot of fun, isn't it? We can play a trick on the bachelors together, what an unruly lot they sound. You can hide in the lounge and use the downstairs cloakroom. I'll bring you some refreshments from the kitchen and then I need to pop out. Make sure you don't go elsewhere in the villa – those boys could be lurking anywhere – definitely don't go in the kitchen, it's a terrible mess, I'll clean it up when I get back.'

*

Tabitha ate the last biscuit on the plate, and Tallulah got up to go into the kitchen to find some more. 'Oh, no, you don't, Tallulah. Miss Mae has been so kind to us. We should obey her orders. Hopefully, she'll be back soon then we can go and make a grand entrance in the pub. It's nearly seven o'clock, we've been in hiding for long enough. I'm getting bored.'

Tabitha went to the downstairs cloakroom, so Tallulah wandered into the kitchen. It didn't look messy. A broken glass had been placed on the worktop near the bin, and the store cupboard door had been left open. The biscuits must be in the store cupboard. Tallulah pushed the door open, and an arm encompassed her, dragging her into the dark.

'So, you've got a soft spot for me.'

'Paddy! What are you doing in Miss Mae's villa? You've broken in, haven't you? Why are you still hanging around?'

'Maybe I'm trying to tame a wild English girl that on the odd occasion pretends to be Irish.'

Tallulah tried to free herself from Paddy's embrace, but he held her tighter. 'I'm going to scream; I'm really going to scream. Tabitha will hear me.'

Paddy's face was near to hers, and his long black hair brushed against her cheeks. 'Is that what you want?'

Tallulah went limp. 'No.'

Time stood still until Tabitha went in search of her sister. 'Oh, my God! What are you doing in here with Paddy? Miss Mae will eat you both alive. We need to go back to the pub before this silly scenario gets out of control. I never wanted to go into hiding, it's just another one of your silly ideas and as far as you're concerned, Paddy, if you come with us without making a fuss, we won't tell Miss Mae that you broke into her villa. The poor woman would be horrified.'

15

BACK AT THE KING ARTHUR

David Makepeace rarely showed emotion; he wasn't sociable or in the least bit friendly. He just kept his head down and did his job. Bringing up four young girls on his own after his beloved Harriet died had been his priority. Of course, he could never have managed without the help of his parents, Arthur and Alice. The girls were all grown up now, and his mother was long gone along with his wife. Maybe that was the problem. There was no woman for David to confide in.

Months ago, David had received a note under the door of his private apartment at the guest house:

The twins are in trouble.

He'd forgotten about it – until now. Another note had arrived this morning:

Watch your back today. Be alert.

*

Back at Villa Elena, Paddy's phone kept vibrating. Tabitha pulled on Tallulah's arm. 'I'm not saying it again! We need to get out of here now. Something doesn't feel right.'

*

Arthur and Clive sat at a table by the window in the pub, while Clive confided in Arthur about the gangland scenario in Paris and the Garibaldi family. Arthur listened but didn't take his eyes off the suspicious character sitting on a barstool at the end of the bar.

Tabitha strode home while Paddy and Tallulah dragged their heels behind her. Tabitha was relieved to have got them out of Villa Elena without too much fuss. Paddy's phone rang, and he answered it. 'It's Miss Mae. I'm in the pub now, the boys are back from Paris, and Bruce Copperfield has just punched Ryan.'

Paddy grinned. He'd given Ryan's photograph to the Copperfield brothers as a decoy. Ryan had kept his back to the bar on his brief visit there the other night. Ryan also had eyes for Tallulah. Paddy had never doubted for a moment that Bruce would floor Ryan. A disturbance, while the real job was carried out was always helpful. From the intelligence now coming through on Paddy's phone, G1 was currently inside the King Arthur and armed with a gun.

In the lane opposite the pub, Paddy pushed Tallulah to the wall, encompassing her in a warm embrace. 'Before I leave, you need to know that your red hair and emerald eyes are more befitting to the Wicklow Mountains than to Paris. Only boys would take you to France; a man would take you to Ireland. I can see you now with the wind in your hair and a pint of Guinness in your hand.'

Tallulah chuckled. 'Could you be getting a soft spot for me?'

Paddy bent down and kissed her firmly on the lips. 'Now that would be telling.'

Tallulah wilted, and Paddy held her by her shoulders while he looked into her eyes. 'All you need to know for now is that you should keep your wits about you. There are people out there you can't trust. Stay away from the pub.'

Paddy kissed the top of Tallulah's head then ran towards the King Arthur.

'Paaaaaddddy!!! Don't leave me.' Tears streamed down Tallulah's face. She had the most terrible feeling in the pit of her stomach that she would never see

Paddy again.

*

David Makepeace had finally found a woman to confide in – Miss Mae. He showed her the note he had received months ago and the one he had received today:

The twins are in trouble.

Watch your back today. Be alert.

Miss Mae squeezed David's hand before winking at him and raising her voice. 'I know you are to be trusted, so I will tell you what I can.'

Arthur pushed past the row that was building between the Copperfield brothers and the bachelors and stood behind the suspicious character seated at the end of the bar who was straining to hear the conversation between Miss Mae and Arthur's son, David. Arthur listened in too.

'There's a gangland boss in Paris who believes his deceased wife, Veronique, had an affair with an English man – about twenty-three years ago. He's recently received photographs of one of your daughters wearing Veronique's Eiffel Tower necklace. So, it all points to one thing. You're the wealthy man that had an affair with Veronique.'

Arthur glanced over at Clive, who was talking to Paddy. The fight at the end of the bar was accelerating, some of the locals had joined in, and it was spilling out onto the street. Tabitha and Tallulah watched in the shadow of a doorway opposite the pub. Things were getting nasty.

David stared Miss Mae in the eyes. 'I never cheated on my Harriet! Who are you to suggest such things?'

Francois Garibaldi leapt onto the bar brandishing a pebblestone candlestick. David Makepeace ducked down, and Arthur held on tightly to the gun he had replaced with one of his artistic creations that were currently being sold in Matilda's shop. France's most wanted man froze at the sight of Arthur pointing a gun at him, and Paddy leapt across the floor to handcuff the elusive G1 before frogmarching him out into the pub garden and over the road to the lane opposite where a van was waiting with Nick in the driving seat.

Ryan and Pete ran back into the pub, through the bar and out into the garden. Ryan stopped briefly to take the gun from Arthur. 'Nice work, Mr Makepeace. Apologies for the fight going on outside.'

Miss Mae took a bottle of brandy and two glasses from behind the bar. 'Let's take a seat, David, I have some explaining to do.'

After pouring the brandies, Miss Mae continued,

with Arthur and Clive straining their ears to listen in to the conversation. 'Now, not all I said was true. I'm sorry you had to get involved with all of that. The twins are safe now, and that's all that matters. That Frenchman was a silly old fool. His son led him to believe that the twins were a product of an affair by his deceased wife, Veronique, and an Englishman. Just because Tallulah got hold of Veronique's necklace, he started imagining all sorts of things. His son was the mastermind in bringing him down by scrambling his mind and using the twins as pawns in his game.'

David gulped the brandy, and Miss Mae topped his glass up. 'Why couldn't his son arrange for him to be captured in France?'

Miss Mae patted David's hand. 'Affairs of the heart, David, my dear. Affairs of the heart. Nothing more powerful to bring a man down. By coming out of hiding to abduct the twins, fleece you of your savings, and then murder you, Francois Garibaldi viewed it as none other than a crime of passion. That's quite acceptable in a Frenchman's eyes. Crime passionnel – it's common in France.'

David knocked the brandy back. 'How did you get involved with all of this?'

Miss Mae stood up and did one of her trademark jigs. 'Oh, let's just say that I've been around a bit. Contacts all over the place. I like to help out where I can.'

David's head was spinning. 'I could have been murdered.'

Miss Mae bent down and threw a strong arm around his shoulders. 'No chance. Paddy's team haven't lost an innocent bystander yet.' Miss Mae had said enough. David wouldn't remember much in the morning. She poured him another brandy just in case. 'Now, did I hear that you're thinking of having a Quiz Night on Tuesdays? Sign me up if that's the case!'

Arthur patted Clive's arm. 'You got away with it. No-one knows about you and Veronique. It's a shame that David had to take the flack, but it all ended well. I think the moral of the story is: Stay away from married women.'

Clive took a large gulp of beer. 'That got a bit scary for a while. I must say that you truly saved the day, Arthur old friend.' Arthur noticed a glint of silver in Clive's clenched fist and nodded towards it. Arthur's eyes bulged when Clive opened his hand to reveal the Eiffel Tower necklace.

'Paddy just gave it to me. He said he had retrieved it from Tallulah when she was partying after the gig race. He thought it should be returned to me. He was very discreet.'

Clive's eyes glistened, and Arthur looked away.

'Nice lad that one. Shame he didn't make the cut at the matchmaking event.'

16

THE BELATED WEDDING RECEPTION

With all the furore of the matchmaking weekend, the day of Hannah and Toby's belated wedding reception arrived in a flash in more ways than one.

For mid-September, the weather was unseasonal. Storm Mirabelle was reaching its peak. The last two days had seen Hannah frantically re-arranging the outdoor event to take place in the large barn instead of on the island in the middle of the lake and surrounding areas. The shallow lake would have been a great paddling pool for the children had the weather been the least bit sunny. How could they keep the children, of all different ages, occupied now for a whole afternoon?

Everyone was getting ready for the event. Changing their high heels for welly boots and trying to find umbrellas that were anything but black, when Miss Mae turned up at the vineyard to offer her services.

'Now, Hannah, you're looking a bit washed out – pardon the pun – with all the clouds opening up as they are outside. Why don't you let me take care of the children today?'

Hannah hugged Miss Mae as she wiped away her tears. 'Anything! Anything at all you can do to help would be most appreciated. Sorry for being such a wet lettuce. It must be my hormones.'

Miss Mae held her shoulders back. 'Now, would I be right in thinking that you have no indoor activities planned?' Hannah shook her head. 'Well, just leave everything to me. Now take a seat while I do your hair. It's so lovely and curly; I think we should leave it down.'

*

The rain was torrential. Matilda and Cindy had given up wearing their long floaty dresses that, when wind-assisted, blew above their heads. Cindy made the final decision. 'This is ridiculous. I'm changing into jeans and a jumper. If anyone gets to the vineyard today, without getting blown into the sea, I'll be amazed.'

Tristan had advised against the helicopter ride for

Clive. So, a two-hour trip in the Bentley from Sonning Hall meant an early start. Clive combed his soaking wet silver blond hair as he jumped into the car. 'We need to pick up Arthur. The weather out there is treacherous.'

Tabitha knocked on Tallulah's bedroom door. 'Are you ready yet? Daddy's ordered a taxi, and we need to leave now!'

There was a group of children around Miss Mae's feet in Hannah's dressing room, and the tension began lifting from Hannah's shoulders. 'I truly believe, Miss Mae, that the best thing I have ever done in my life, was recruiting you to be the manager of Little Finchies & Friends.'

Miss Mae waved a hand in the air. 'You're far too kind, Hannah.'

'Do you think the storm's a sign, Miss Mae? Is it a sign that I've made the wrong decision marrying Toby?'

Miss Mae looked out of the window at the black clouds and forks of lightning. 'The storm is definitely a sign; it means that something's in need of a good shake-up. I can guarantee it's not to do with you and Toby, Hannah. You two have just started out on your journey together – you've found your destiny.' A smiling Miss Mae turned around to face Hannah.

'Trust me, there will be a surprising change before the storm passes.'

*

By two o'clock, all the guests were drying out in the barn. Will Tomlin had driven Lady Leticia from the chateau, and Miss Mae was planning to avoid the Lady at all costs; she hadn't seen her since the matchmaking event, and she was sure Leticia would want a de-brief to analyse why the event went so wrong.

So far, Miss Mae had protected Paddy's team as best as she could. The twins and David Makepeace just wanted to forget all about the unfortunate incident involving a gangster. Miss Mae had advised them that it was Gangland Code of Practice in France not to speak about such events and, if any details got out, then Arthur would be at risk of revenge as his fingerprints were on Francois Garibaldi's gun. Everyone agreed that it was best to protect Arthur.

At two-thirty, Toby clinked a glass from the balcony inside the barn. 'Ladies, Gentlemen and children, I have stood here many times before, at charity events and social occasions. Until now, I have always been alone. Well, from now and for evermore, I am *not* alone. Please be upstanding to welcome my beautiful wife, Hannah Makepeace.'

Hannah glided into the barn, on the arm of her

father, David Makepeace. She wore a long ivory dress. The emerald bracelet Toby had given her when they first met was glittering on her wrist, and her long curly black hair was covered in raindrops. A drenched Miss Mae followed behind, shaking out an umbrella.

Everyone stood up and applauded at the sight of Hannah and her father, making their way to the bottom of the balcony steps. Toby ran down the steps and took Hannah's hand to help her on the climb to join him. When she reached the balcony, she kissed Toby to cheers and whistles from the crowd below.

Hannah smiled down at their guests. 'Toby and I can't thank you all enough for coming here today in this terrible weather. As you know, I'm not big on tradition. I just want you all to have a lovely afternoon with lots of food and endless Finchinglake wine.'

There were more cheers. Toby nodded to Hannah's bouquet and winked at his wife. 'Oh, well, there's just one tradition I might succumb to. Hannah turned her back to the crowd and threw the flowers over her shoulder into the sea of raised arms below. She turned to see that the lucky recipient was Will Tomlin. He waved the bouquet in the air with one hand and pushed his glasses up his nose with the other.

Toby laughed. 'If you're planning on getting married, Will, then find a local girl. There's no way I'm going to risk my accountant moving away.'

Lady Leticia made a mental note. The next matchmaking event should cater for Will. She had taken him under her wing as the son she'd never had. He was living in the grounds of the chateau in Hannah's old house, and Leticia loved having him around. She wished she'd thought of the idea sooner instead of wasting her time with the twins. Leticia pushed her guilty secret to the back of her mind. There was no need to break the news to Will yet that he was descended from the original Lord of the chateau. No need at all.

Will kept checking his phone for weather reports. He showed the latest projection to Toby. 'If the eye of storm Mirabelle hits us as predicted tonight, this barn won't be standing.'

Toby squeezed Will's shoulder. 'Keep me updated, Will. I don't want to worry Hannah.'

Miss Mae produced a bag of balloons and proceeded to make animals on demand for the children. She had karaoke planned for later, and games of pin the tail on the donkey and musical chairs.

Tallulah pulled on Matilda's sleeve. 'You know you saw that vision of me running through fields with a pint glass, well could you have another look into the emerald pram and see if you can find one of the bachelors? His name is Paddy, he has long black hair and bright blue eyes, and he's Irish.'

Matilda reached for her phone, then handed it to Matilda. 'Is this him?'

Tallulah stared at the photograph of Paddy, Ryan and Pete and Matilda giggled. 'Cindy and I shared a very nice evening with Paddy in the King Arthur, the day he got disqualified.'

Lady Leticia grabbed the phone. 'Show me that! What were Baron Pigstrotter and George William doing in the King Arthur with Paddy when they should have been at the chateau wooing the twins? They were fortunate to get through to the final six. Neither of them was my choice; they were both Miss Mae's.'

Miss Mae took the phone from the Lady and handed it back to a confused Matilda, not before "accidentally" pressing "delete". 'Oh, boys will be boys. There's no Guinness at the chateau; they probably popped down to the pub to have a little commiseration drink with Paddy.'

Miss Mae winked at Tallulah and linked arms with Leticia before leading her towards the buffet table. 'Let's not talk about that unfortunate event any more. I should never have got involved. It all went belly-up because of my bad choice in men. No wonder I've never been married.'

Matilda stared at Tallulah, who shrugged her shoulders. 'Tallulah! What's going on?'

Tallulah sighed. 'You'd never believe me if I tried to explain. All I'll say is that not all of the bachelors were who they said they were. The only genuine one is Paddy. It's doing my head in, Tilly. I need to find him.'

17

IN THE EYE OF THE STORM

Storm Mirabelle continued throughout the afternoon, and several of the guests huddled together on hay bales in the far corner of the barn to keep warm. Tabitha was startled by a knee in her back. 'Oh, for goodness sake, keep to your own space. Just leave me alone.'

An inebriated Will Tomlin had the confidence to air what had been niggling him for the last couple of weeks. 'You can't talk. What were you doing chasing after that male model? You didn't leave *him* alone. Lady Leticia tried so hard to find bachelors for you and Tallulah. Well, she shouldn't have wasted her time. One sight of Posterius and you were off up to his room.'

Tabitha turned around. 'How dare you make such accusations! You're a nobody. You work at the vineyard during the day as Toby's accountant, and then you go home to Hannah's old house in the grounds of the chateau and let Lady Leticia treat you like a son. You've got it good, Will Tomlin. You've seriously got it good.'

There was a clap of thunder, and Tabitha threw her arms around Will. 'Do you think we will die in here?'

Will pulled Tabitha towards him and stroked her mass of long curly red hair. 'No chance. Now, I'm intrigued to know why you're wearing a palm tree necklace. Have you ever seen palm trees in real life before?'

A lightning strike, followed by more thunder and wind whipping through the barn made Tabitha grip Will more tightly. 'Yes, I definitely have, in Torquay once.'

Will took his chance. 'This will sound very forward, but I'm not very good with girlfriends, I've just been dumped yet again. The problem is, I have a holiday booked in the Caribbean in January. Would you like to come with me? If nothing else, you could give me lessons on girls.'

Tabitha gripped Will so tightly he struggled to

breathe. 'Of course, I will. What do I have to lose? The weather's always rubbish in Truelove Hills in January.'

*

Arthur and Clive sat on plastic chairs and clung onto wooden tables. Arthur held Fluffy tight; he wished he'd taken his little dog to safety into the main building.

Tallulah crawled along the floor, sheltering from the powering wind that was blasting through from the broken barn door. She reached Matilda and Theo, who were cradling a sleeping Mollie. 'Are we going to die in here? You should know, Tilly. You know everything with your "visions".'

A thunderbolt of lightning struck a metal bin outside the barn and sparks shot high into the sky.

Toby had waited long enough for the storm to subside, but it wasn't passing, it was just getting worse. He had to ensure the safety of his guests so he rallied the support of Jamie, Theo and Will and began devising an action plan of how to evacuate the barn without sustaining any casualties.

Within five minutes, Miss Mae pointed to the weather-beaten barn door. 'How lovely, Hannah, it's brightening up out there. It can take a good storm to ruffle a few feathers, clear away the cobwebs, open the eyes of young lovers.'

Before Hannah could make sense of a tipsy Miss Mae's ramblings, she was joined by an incredulous Toby. 'Would you believe it? The sun's out! I was just about to evacuate the barn. I'll check to see if the sound system's working again. It's time to party!'

Miss Mae dragged David Makepeace onto the dancefloor and held him close. 'It must be very difficult for you, David, not having a woman to confide in. Tell me your deepest worries.'

David held his head back and straightened his shoulders, ensuring he didn't come into contact with Miss Mae any more than was necessary. 'It's the twins. Especially now that Hannah and Matilda are married off. They'll remain my responsibility until they find partners to protect them. Just look at the escapades they've been involved in since you've been around.'

Miss Mae nodded in agreement. 'Do you think there will come a time when you're ready to move on from your wife?'

David pushed Miss Mae away. The conversation was getting much too personal for his liking. 'Definitely not! No-one will replace Harriet.'

As they headed towards the drinks table, Miss Mae couldn't resist a thought; David was cut from the same cloth as Arthur. Arthur had never moved on from Alice. There were some occasions where Miss Mae couldn't lend a helping hand.

David poured himself a large glass of Finchinglake Pinot Noir and Miss Mae patted him on the back before she was whisked away by Will Tomlin.

Will spoke in a low voice. 'She said "yes"! She's going with me to the Caribbean.'

Miss Mae winked and gave a thumbs up. Sometimes men just needed a little help. She'd seen a protective Will watching Tabitha during the recent matchmaking event. Now there was a match that had potential. All it takes is a little creativity to get things started. That emerald palm tree necklace of Tabitha's was a perfect conversation starter. Miss Mae hoped that Will booked the Caribbean trip soon. Tabitha wouldn't mind a little white lie once she'd fallen for Will.

18

A LASTING LOVE

The next morning, Miss Mae's eyes twinkled as she planned her next move. She dialled a number on her phone and waited for the recipient to pick up. 'Oh, hello, Clive. It's Miss Mae. I need a little favour. I know you're a bit of a romantic. Let me share my thoughts with you.'

*

Tallulah sat on a chair inside Matilda's shop and refused to move. 'Why hasn't he contacted me? It's been over two weeks. You need to help me, Tilly, look into the emerald pram and get a vision. Pleeeease! What's Paddy up to now?'

Matilda sighed and took the pram out of her bag. She'd taken it off the windowsill in Mollie's room this morning before leaving for work. She'd been expecting a visit from Tallulah. 'I can't just look into the pram to find a missing person. As Hannah said: "Emeralds are believed to foretell future events and reveal one's truths." You're expecting too much of me, Tallulah. What if I see something you won't like? Would you want to know?'

Tallulah shifted in her seat. 'I want to know everything. Just have a look, will you? Pleeeease.'

Matilda changed the sign on the shop door to "CLOSED" and gave her full concentration to the emerald pram. She stared into it for fifteen minutes before putting the pram away in her bag.

'Well, what did you see?'

'Nothing, just nothing.'

Tallulah jumped up and made her way over the road to the pub. She was already an hour late for her shift. Bruce Copperfield was wiping tables and replacing beer mats. He didn't look up when she breezed in without so much as an excuse or apology. Tallulah was suspicious. 'Why aren't you moaning? Aren't you even bothered that I'm late? Why are you ignoring me, Bruce Copperfield?'

Bruce picked up the cleaning bucket and took it into the pub garden before wiping the tables out there.

Steve Copperfield was sniggering, and Tallulah stood with hands on hips. 'What's going on, are *you* going to tell me?'

Steve carried on polishing glasses with a wide grin on his face. 'You'll never believe what's just happened. Those bachelors are back. They stormed in here like they owned the place. Two of them held onto Bruce while another punched him. He'll have a real shiner come opening time. To top that, the one that threw the punch said that they were now "quits" and shook Bruce's hand. They said they'd be back for a pint later before asking the direction to Pebble Peak.'

Tallulah rushed to the door. 'How long ago was this?'

'Oh, about half an hour ago. They had bags with them, so I'm guessing they've booked to stay in the glamping huts.'

A switch flicked in Tallulah's mind. Why hadn't she thought of it before? The vision that Matilda had seen was of Tallulah running through a field with a pint glass. Matilda said it was very green. Tallulah's future was connected to Pebble Peak! Paddy had come back for her! Tallulah was in a daze, and she approached Steve with sparkling eyes. She kissed him firmly on the lips before taking hold of the pint glass he was polishing. 'You've made me so happy, Steve. You'll never know how much. I don't know if or when I'll be back. Please cover for me.'

Steve watched Tallulah gliding up the High Street towards Pebble Peak. He wiped his mouth with the back of his hand and glanced at Bruce, who was still cleaning tables in the garden. What had just happened?

*

Matilda couldn't get the vision she had just seen in the emerald pram out of her mind. A much younger Miss Mae was in a nurse's uniform. She was waving her arms about and appeared to be distressed. Matilda sensed tragedy. There was a body on a hospital trolley shrouded in black. The vision flickered before it was gone.

*

Tallulah had reached Pebble Peak. She danced around the lake at the top and smiled at the startled ducks. The wind blew her hair over her face, and she held the pint glass aloft before calling: 'Paddy! Paddy, you came back.'

The door to a glamping hut opened, and Nick, Ryan and Pete emerged. Tallulah pulled her hair away from her eyes. 'Where's Paddy?'

Pete smiled. 'We've no idea where Paddy is. We had to come back for Ryan's sake. He's just settled things with that moody bloke in the pub. He had to learn a lesson that he can't just go around punching anyone for no good reason.'

Tallulah fell onto the grass, and the pint glass rolled into a bush. Ryan knelt next to her. 'Are you in need of the kiss of life?'

Tallulah continued to lie flat on her back. 'Not from Mr Piggy, I'm not.' Tallulah stared at the sky. What a let-down. A glimmer of hope had turned her into some sort of floating fairy. What was wrong with her? She couldn't even remember climbing up to Pebble Peak. She closed her eyes and lay still. She just wanted the world to go away.

Pete glanced at Nick. 'Do you think she's all right? She didn't faint. She just collapsed in a heap like the stuffing had gone out of her.'

Nick chuckled. 'I could always wake her up by taking my shirt off and jogging around the lake. She won't be able to resist a bit of "Posterius".'

Tallulah stirred. 'Oh, no! Oh, no, oh no!' She jumped up. 'I have to get back to work. How am I going to explain that I kissed Steve Copperfield? Just wait until I see Paddy again. I'll be giving him a piece of my mind. How can he keep a girl waiting like this?'

*

Miss Mae sat down on the end of her bed. She was

most disturbed that, following the capture of G2 in Paris she couldn't get hold of Paddy. The good news was that Francois Garibaldi the second was now behind bars and the Garibaldi gangland scenario was defunct. The bad news was that Paddy was missing.

19

MISSING

In the pub that lunchtime, Clive confided in Arthur about Miss Mae. 'I'm concerned, Arthur. I have a feeling that Miss Mae is trying to gain my affection. She's been acting very strangely.'

Arthur twisted his moustache. 'She's always been strange, that one. What makes you think she's after you?'

'Well, she wanted to make me lunch the other week. She practically dragged me into Villa Elena. Fortunately, she's not a good cook; she burned the sausages. I escaped that bizarre episode scot-free. However, I took a call from her this morning that left me feeling very uncomfortable.'

'What did she say?'

'Something about me being "a bit of a romantic". She said she'd never been to Ireland and she'd never been in a private jet. She then went on about making a woman very happy and asked if I'd take her there.'

'Damn cheek. If you ask me, she just wants a free lift to Ireland. I see what you mean though about feeling uncomfortable. I hope you said "no".'

'That's just the point, Arthur. I couldn't say "no". I was taken by surprise, and Jamie and Cindy have always praised Miss Mae's efforts in looking after Sebastian. I felt I owed her something for taking such good care of my grandson. She said we could be there and back in a day if we leave early enough. I weighed things up and thought it was the most gentlemanly thing to do to accompany her.'

'When are you going?'

'Tomorrow.'

*

The bachelors arrived at the pub from Pebble Peak, and Ryan placed the empty pint glass on the bar in front of Tallulah. Bruce glared at him through his one good eye. 'Three pints of your finest ale, please, Tallulah.'

Miss Mae entered the pub and gave a wink and a little wave to Clive before striding over to join the bachelors. She looked over her shoulder before whispering: 'Where's Paddy?'

Pete shrugged. 'We haven't seen him since G2 was captured yesterday. It got pretty scary for a while, but we're out of there now, and Paddy's obviously gone on to pastures new. The girls are classy in Paris; he may have stayed on for a bit of adventure of his own.'

Miss Mae frowned. 'Well, I'm worried about him. He's not answering my calls. I'm going over to Ireland tomorrow so I'll keep my ear to the ground for intelligence.'

Bruce Copperfield's anger was escalating. Steve knew when things were about to erupt. 'Calm down, Bruce. You hit the guy in the first place. That wasn't what Paddy asked you to do; he asked you to call him.'

Tallulah's ears pricked up from the far end of the bar and Bruce narrowed his eyes. 'If I ever find out that Tallulah kissed him, I'll kill him.'

Steve shot a worried glance at Tallulah, who raised her eyes. Steve wiped his mouth again and excused himself to go to the lavatory. He needed to look in a mirror. What if Tallulah had been wearing lipstick this morning? He needed to check.

Miss Mae said her goodbyes to the bachelors and grabbed Clive's shoulder on her way out. 'I'll be waiting for you at six o'clock in the morning outside Villa

Elena. I must admit I'm quite excited. I can quite guarantee that you're going to have the time of your life. I must go now. I need to get my beauty sleep.'

Arthur looked at his watch. It was only three o'clock in the afternoon. That woman was unbelievable. Clive had turned a worrying shade of grey. Arthur signalled to Tallulah at the bar by waving two fingers in the air. Tallulah pulled two pints and took them over to her grandfather before going in search of Steve. 'Steve, I heard you say to Bruce that he should have called Paddy. Do you have Paddy's number?'

Steve scratched his head. 'I'm trying to remember where I put his card. Bruce threw it in the bin, but I took it out in case we ever needed it. Now, where did I put it for safekeeping?'

Tallulah stifled a scream. Stupid boy. She'd search high and low for Paddy's card. Where would Steve have put it so that Bruce wouldn't find it? She rushed behind the bar and pulled out the crate the twins stood on if they couldn't reach the top shelves. She grabbed a cloth and pretended to dust high and low.

One hour later the pub door opened and David Makepeace arrived with boxes of snacks from the wholesalers. His eyes widened at the sight of Tallulah standing on a windowsill dusting around the window frame. Clive stood up and walked over to David. 'We're very concerned about Tallulah. She seems to have lost it, so to speak. She keeps muttering "I can't find it, I will find it, I will find it if it kills me". Arthur tried talking to her, but she's on a mission about something.'

David put the boxes on the floor and helped his daughter down from the windowsill. 'Come with me next door to the guest house. I'll make you a cup of tea.'

Tallulah let out an excited cry. 'The guest house! I haven't checked the guest house!' She ran out of the pub with her father in hot pursuit.

'What are you looking for, Tallulah?'

'Paddy's card. He left a card with his number on it. Bruce threw it away, and Steve hid it somewhere. Now he can't remember where it is.'

David took out his wallet and produced the card. 'I found this on top of the microwave in the pub kitchen. I had a feeling I should keep hold of it. Is this what you're looking for?'

Tallulah hugged her father. 'You're the best daddy in the whole wide world. Can you cover for me in the pub while I make a phone call? The queue's a bit long, and Bruce is in one of his strops. An extra pair of hands is just what the boys need.'

20

IRELAND

On arrival at Dublin airport, Clive unclasped his seatbelt and glanced out of the window of the private jet. 'What a lovely day for our visit to Ireland, Miss Mae. Do you have an itinerary for our brief stay?'

Miss Mae twisted the strap on her shoulder bag between her busy fingers. She needed to stop doing that, the stitching was becoming quite worn. Why wasn't Paddy returning her calls? There was only one thing for it, she'd have to carry on regardless and wish for the best. 'Well, I've been told that you can't come to Ireland without visiting the Wicklow Mountains. We should go there first.'

Tristan ran down the steps onto the tarmac and opened the doors of the waiting limousine. Once Clive and Miss Mae were in the back, he jumped into the front seat and, on Miss Mae's instruction, headed for County Wicklow.

Clive was enjoying the experience; Miss Mae was never short of conversation – she was indeed an intelligent woman. Neither of them had been to Ireland before, and they were fascinated by the greenery and vastness of space. Driving through small villages of grey ramshackle buildings, with the occasional thatched roof, Clive felt as if he had been taken back in time. Even the towns were sleepy; ruined castles and forts perched beside rivers, and swathes of orange bracken brought contrasting colour to the endless green landscape.

Clive leant forward and peered out of the window. 'My goodness, Miss Mae. Can you see over there? There's the most beautiful lake, with the backdrop of the mountains behind it. It's pure joy to behold.'

Miss Mae knocked on the glass window that separated Tristan from his passengers, and he spoke through a microphone into speakers in the back of the limousine. Miss Mae shot back into her seat. 'Now that we're in the Wicklow Mountains, there's an address we need to find.'

Clive raised an eyebrow. 'I thought we were just

having a little trip out here from the airport. I had presumed we'd head straight back to Dublin and take in the history and architecture. I am looking forward to tasting a pint of Guinness in its true homeland. I've been told there's nothing quite like it.'

Miss Mae ignored Clive and read out an address for Tristan. 'I hope you can find it. They're not very good with postcodes or house numbers around here. It's a bit remote.'

Twenty minutes later, and high up in the mountains, the limousine stood outside a pair of electric gates. Miss Mae jumped out of the back seat and punched in a code on a keypad. The gates opened slowly, allowing Miss Mae enough time to jump back in. Tristan manoeuvred the large vehicle up a steep winding driveway. Clive's heart raced at the sight of the sheer drop outside the car window. Miss Mae knocked on the glass window again. 'Watch the clutch, Tristan, make sure you don't burn it out. We wouldn't want to get stranded around here.'

Miss Mae checked her phone. There was still no news from Paddy. Where was he? Tristan parked outside a large glass-fronted house built into the side of a mountain. Clive and Miss Mae climbed out of the car. Clive breathed in the aroma of the Wicklow Mountains – the scent of the woodland mixed with burning peat. 'This is a most wonderful place, Miss Mae. Do you know the people who live here?'

Miss Mae did a little jig. 'Yes, I do, Clive. And so, do you.'

Clive and Tristan wandered around the garden admiring the view, and Miss Mae knocked on the front door of the house. A hand grabbed her, pulled her inside and slammed the door. 'What did you bring him here for? I've been tricked.'

Miss Mae smoothed the sleeve of her jacket and took a moment to register Veronique's outburst. 'I was just trying to do a little bit of matchmaking. Now that your gangster family's behind bars, you can come out of hiding.'

Veronique paced around the glass-fronted hallway, taking care to stay out of Clive's line of sight. He was busy chatting to his driver and oblivious to her. 'He's changed, Miss Mae. He's old now. You should have told me you were planning this rather than getting me over here for a little holiday while my husband and son were arrested. I want to go back to Canada; I have lots of friends amongst the French expatriates, and lots of admirers too. I am very happy, Miss Mae, I do not wish to drag up the past.'

Miss Mae raised her hands in the air. 'But, Veronique, you are the love of Clive's life. It was unfortunate that we had to fake your death all those years ago, it was far too dangerous for you to stay in France. You have an opportunity now to rekindle your love affair with Clive, and I am helping to make that happen.'

Veronique tutted. 'I will not let him see me. I am old now too. I have wrinkles, and I am two kilos heavier than when he last held me in his arms. Just look at my hair – it's short and spikey and purple! Clive used to love my long blonde hair; he said it felt like gossamer.'

Miss Mae looked closely at Veronique. She couldn't spot a wrinkle; she couldn't spot any expression on Veronique's face either. She sighed; Clive wouldn't be taken with his beloved Veronique succumbing to Botox. Her planned reunion was turning into a complete and utter disaster.

Veronique pushed Miss Mae towards the front door. 'You have been very good to me over the years, but I am self-sufficient now. You are best going back to being a nurse in Paris. Yes, you should go there and leave me to my own life now.'

Miss Mae suppressed a sob. 'Well, pack your bags, Veronique. Paddy's due home any day now, and he only gave me the use of his home while he was away.'

Veronique reached for a phone on the hall table. 'This phone keeps ringing. It was in the bedside drawer and kept disturbing my sleep, so I brought it out here. I think your Paddy friend may have forgotten to take it with him.'

Miss Mae put the phone in her bag. 'Goodbye, Veronique. I am pleased your life has had a happy ending.'

The door closed behind Miss Mae, and she signalled to Clive and Tristan to get back into the limousine.

Miss Mae was quiet on the way back to Dublin; she kept blowing her nose and blaming it on the trees in the Wicklow Mountains. She said she must have an allergy to Ireland and that she was keen to get home. She didn't want the day to be a total disappointment for Clive so she asked Tristan to drop them off in the Temple Bar area on the South Bank of the River Liffey so that Clive could have a pint of Guinness – she needed one herself.

It was noisy in the pub; Miss Mae struggled to hear Clive over the enthusiastic fiddle player and the lively crowd. 'What did you say, Clive?'

'I said: Who lives in that house in the Wicklow Mountains that we both know?'

Miss Mae downed her second pint. 'Oh, Paddy, that's all. He wasn't at home today, though.'

Clive finished his second pint too and stood up to go to the bar. 'That's a shame. It was lucky his maid was around to let you in for a chat. Shocking hair colour for a woman of her age. Still, each to their own.'

While Clive was at the bar, Miss Mae delved into her bag and took out the phone. It was definitely Paddy's phone; there were several missed calls from her and nineteen from Tallulah. Miss Mae phoned Tallulah.

'Paddy!!! Why haven't you been answering my calls?'

Miss Mae took a deep breath. 'It's me, Tallulah, Miss Mae. I'm over in Ireland at the moment, and I've just picked up Paddy's phone. Would you like to leave a message?'

Tallulah stamped her foot. That woman was everywhere. At least she knew where Paddy was at the moment; he was back home in Ireland, and he'd been ignoring her calls. He'd much rather hang out with Miss Mae than with her and, by the noise in the background, they were having a whale of a time. Tallulah ended the call. She had better things to do than hang her hopes on a loser.

21

LUNCH AT THE CHATEAU

The following morning, David Makepeace received another note under the door to his private apartment in the guest house. This time the note read:

Meet me for lunch at the chateau. 1.00 pm.

David sighed. Miss Mae was back. That woman just didn't know when to stop. He'd made it clear that he wasn't interested. Still, he supposed she meant no harm. It wasn't his fault that he was still attractive in his fifties. David looked in the mirror at his black curly hair, green eyes and bushy eyebrows and pushed his chest out. All that lugging of beer barrels and crates had kept him fit. He was still a fine figure of a man.

David was sure the writing on the note was the same as the others. He placed the new note next to the other two just to check:

The twins are in trouble.

Watch your back today. Be alert.

Meet me for lunch at the chateau. 1.00 pm.

Yes, the notes had all been written by the same person. Maybe Miss Mae wasn't so bad, after all. If he was honest, he had to admit that she'd tried to protect the twins and even him. He owed it to her to turn up at the chateau at lunchtime and let her down gently.

*

Tabitha was relieved that Tallulah had finally come down to earth after swooning over Paddy. She seemed much more amiable today and had even agreed to cover Tabitha's lunchtime shift at the pub. Tabitha hadn't mentioned to her twin that she was going to the Caribbean in January with Will Tomlin. She could hardly believe it herself. Still, it was best to wait until she had more details and Will had invited her for lunch at the chateau at 12.45 pm to discuss the arrangements.

*

Nick, Ryan and Pete were packing their bags in the glamping hut. Ryan looked out of the window. 'Nice little place this, off the beaten track. I must say that our latest mission has been quite enjoyable on occasions.'

Pete zipped up his rucksack. 'The highlight for me was when I was given the name "George William", and you two were called "Baron Pigstrotter" and "Posterius".'

The men burst into fits of giggles. Ryan grinned at Nick. 'So, "Posterius", what was your highlight?'

Nick scratched his head. 'Now let me think – there were many. It's the lowlight that will stick out in my mind though – when that dog peed up my leg!'

More laughter and Pete nodded towards Ryan. 'What was your highlight?'

Ryan's eyes twinkled. 'Coming back here to give a right hook to that bloke behind the bar. I've no idea why he went for me in the first place. Still, I'm happy now I've settled the score. He'll have a right shiner for a few days.'

*

Tabitha held her long curly red hair up on one side and secured it with a silver clip. It matched the silver of her necklace, and the emerald leaves of the palm tree charm matched the colour of her eyes. She chose to wear a cream fitted dress. She hoped it wasn't too posh for lunch or too cold for September, so she reached for a pale green pashmina and threw it around her shoulders before making her way up the High Street to the chateau.

*

Will Tomlin had arrived in the restaurant early. He'd combed his thick light brown hair into a side parting, and the fringe kept falling into his eyes. Still, he didn't have to worry about knocking off his glasses when he brushed it back; he'd made the rare effort to wear contact lenses. Living in the chateau grounds with Lady Leticia encouraging him to have full access to the chateau's facilities, Will knew all the staff. Although the restaurant was busy this lunchtime, Will had managed to secure the most private table on the mezzanine floor with views of the sea.

Gerard, the butler, showed Tabitha to her seat. 'Wow, Will! This is amazing. I've never been up here before. Are these tables more expensive to book? Ooops, sorry, shouldn't have asked that.'

Gerard arrived with an ice bucket, and Will pushed his fringe out of his eyes. 'I hope you like champagne.'

Tabitha turned around from draping her pashmina over the back of her chair. 'Ooooh, yes! Thank you, Will.'

'Well, here's a toast to us and our Caribbean holiday!'

'Yes, let's toast to that. How lovely!'

Tabitha sipped her champagne and took a good look at Will. He looked different. It was obvious that he wasn't wearing glasses, but there was something else. Had he styled his hair differently? Tabitha wasn't sure; she hadn't had a good look at him before. He was rather attractive, and she suddenly felt very nervous. 'Would you excuse me for a moment, Will? I need to pop to the cloakroom. If Gerard comes back while I'm gone, then please order me soup for starters.'

Swinging her hips and puffing up her hair, Tallulah hoped she looked good from behind. She only needed to get down the steps to ground level without falling flat on her face then she could retreat to the cloakroom to compose herself and touch up her lipstick.

Tabitha strode past the reception area just as her father walked in. 'Daddy! What are you doing here? Why are you wearing your best suit?'

David Makepeace fiddled with his tie. 'I could ask you the same. About why you're here, that is.'

Tabitha blushed. 'Well, I'm here on a sort of date. It's not a real date. You could say that I'm meeting an acquaintance.'

David shuffled his feet. 'The same.'

Tabitha wasn't letting this go. 'What do you mean "the same"? Who are you meeting for lunch?'

David shrugged his shoulders. 'It's nothing to get excited about. It's only Miss Mae. The poor woman's lonely. After everything she's done in the village, the least I can do is give her an hour of my time.'

Tabitha winked then kissed her father on the cheek. 'Don't do anything I wouldn't do.'

David watched his daughter stride into the cloakroom then steeled himself to enter the restaurant to find Miss Mae. Despite scanning the whole room, he couldn't see her anywhere. He checked his watch: 1.05 pm. Miss Mae was never late for anything. A voice sounded from the far side of the room. 'Mr Makepeace, I'm at the table over here.'

David spun around and was stunned to see a waving Paddy. Paddy stood up and held out his hand to shake David's. 'Thank you for joining me for lunch today.'

David pulled out a chair and sat down. 'Have *you* been writing the notes?'

'Of course. Who else would you be expecting to have lunch with on such a fine day?' Paddy chuckled. 'Well, OK, I guess you didn't expect it to be me.'

David held his head in his hands: *Watch your back. The twins are in trouble.* Now he thought back to it; it made sense that it was Paddy who was trying to protect him and the girls. He shook his head to clear his thoughts of Miss Mae. She wasn't interested in him after all. He didn't know whether to be relieved or disappointed.

Tabitha couldn't resist a sneaky look in the dining room. What if they were holding hands? She peered into the restaurant, and her hand flew to her mouth. Her father had lied to her. He wasn't meeting Miss Mae; he was meeting Paddy! She turned and ran up the steps to join Will.

'You'll never guess what's just happened. I've just had the fright of my life. Is there any chance of a pint of cider to calm my nerves?'

Will reached over the table and held Tabitha's hand. 'Of course, I much prefer cider to champagne too. You should have said.'

Once David Makepeace had got over the initial shock, he sensed that Paddy was nervous.

'Now, Mr Makepeace, I'm here today for one thing only. I'm an old-fashioned soul, and I need your approval for my next mission.'

Three pints of cider later and Tabitha realised what it was about Will that she couldn't quite put her finger on earlier. 'You know the hallway in the chateau with all the portraits? You look just like one of the previous Lords. You have the same unusual eyes.'

Will's smile faded. 'I've seen the one. His eyes are a strange colour, aren't they? They can only be described as muddy brown. I try to hide mine behind my glasses. I've got them in my pocket; I'll pop them back on.'

Tabitha grabbed both of Will's hands. 'Oh, no! Don't do that. I love the colour of your eyes. You look so much better without your glasses. Nice hairstyle, by the way, it's adorable when you keep running your fingers through your fringe.'

Gerard coughed. 'Excuse me, but the restaurant has now been closed for an hour.'

Will winked at Tabitha. 'Shall we continue our conversation back at my house?'

Tabitha grinned and grabbed her pashmina. She couldn't even remember what they'd been discussing. They hadn't gone into the detail of their Caribbean holiday yet. And whatever her father was up to was his business. For once in her life, Tabitha had more exciting things to focus on.

22

THE NEXT MISSION

David Makepeace went straight from the chateau to the pub. He handed an envelope to Tallulah. 'I've been feeling a bit sorry for you these last few days. Especially now that Tabitha's got fixed up with Will Tomlin and he's taking her to the Caribbean.'

Tallulah's emerald eyes flared. 'What? Never in a million years would Tabitha take off with Will Tomlin and go to the Caribbean without checking with me first. We're twins! Who told you?'

David tried not to laugh; it was always easy to wind Tallulah up. 'Miss Mae told me the other day. I didn't believe it myself until I just saw them with my own eyes having lunch at the chateau.'

Tallulah kicked the crate below the bar. 'What?! I'm

covering her shift!'

David nodded to the envelope that Tallulah was waving around in the air. 'Well, aren't you going to open it?'

Tallulah ripped the envelope open. 'One-way flight ticket to Dublin. You're having a laugh, aren't you?'

'Not at all. Miss Mae was in Dublin yesterday, and she said that the service in the pub she went to with Clive was appalling. She said that you should go over there and sort things out. That's why it's a one-way ticket. We don't know how long you'll need to sort things out.'

'But the flight leaves in the morning.'

'That should be enough time for you to pack a few things. I'll make sure Tabitha pulls her weight while you're away. She asked a bit much of you to cover her shift and not even mention she was going on a hot date. If you want to go and do your packing, I'll cover for you this afternoon. Don't worry about accommodation when you get to Ireland, that's all sorted.'

Tallulah's heart sank. Her twin sister was with Will Tomlin. She was now officially the last of the Makepeace girls to find love. She was left on the shelf. A spinster for evermore like Mrs Carruthers and Miss Mae. What had she got to lose by sorting out a rubbish pub in Dublin? At least she wouldn't have to listen to Tabitha chattering on about the Caribbean and swooning over Will. If she was honest with herself, this change had come at just the right time.

*

Tabitha dragged her case through the Arrivals hall at Dublin airport. She searched for her name on the boards held aloft by taxi drivers and chauffeurs. It wasn't long before she spotted it. A six-foot-tall leprechaun was dancing around waving a sign in the air:

TALLULAH
my
TRUELOVE

Tallulah thumped the leprechaun on his arm. 'You couldn't even get my name right. I'm Tallulah Makepeace from Truelove Hills in England. Do you work in the pub too? Well, I'm not very impressed with the welcome you've concocted for me. Knowing my luck, you've got me scheduled on for a double shift, starting from lunchtime.'

The leprechaun smiled and took hold of Tallulah's case. She had no choice but to follow him. On the fourth floor of the car park, he unlocked the doors of a rusty old car. Tallulah had never seen one like it. She climbed into the back seat and lifted her case onto the seat beside her.

There were several ways out of Dublin airport; to the North, to the West, to the South, to the City Centre. Tallulah was grateful for one thing; it wouldn't be a long journey to the City Centre. She closed her eyes and listened to the tinny sound of Irish music coming from the radio. She didn't want to open her eyes in case she spotted a hole in the floor or a dead rat under her seat. With all the trauma of the last few days, Tallulah fell asleep.

'Well, are ye going to get out now or what? To be sure, I've given in to being dressed up as a leprechaun, but it's taking it a bit far to get my mean machine up that drive.'

Tallulah woke with a start. 'Is this the pub?'

The leprechaun laughed. 'Of course not. It's where you're staying. Mind yourself on the way up; it's a sheer drop down to the right.'

The electric gates closed behind Tallulah, and she dragged her case up the drive. When she reached the glass-fronted house built into the side of a mountain, there was a note pinned to the door.

Come on in. It's unlocked.
Make your way to the kitchen.

Tallulah's heart pounded. She walked into the

kitchen and noticed an open store cupboard door. She crept towards it. She pushed it further ajar, and her heart sank. There was no-one inside.

A noise from behind alarmed her, and she spun around to the sight of Paddy leaning against the kitchen door with his arms folded. 'Now, why would I be hiding in a cupboard in my very own house?' Tears streamed down Tallulah's face, and Paddy walked over to embrace her. 'To be sure, why would a girl I have a soft spot for, be so heartbroken?'

Tallulah sobbed into his chest. 'I'm not heartbroken; I'm just so happy.'

*

The leprechaun sat on a bench beside a lake at the foot of the Wicklow Mountains. He checked his watch then wandered down the road to a pub. If nothing else, he knew that Paddy kept precision timing.

*

Tallulah dried her eyes and blew her nose before grabbing Paddy's hand. 'You need to take me to a pub. I need to run through a field with a pint glass in my hand. When I've done that our future will be sealed and my dreams will come true.'

Paddy raised his eyebrows. 'Now, you're going to have to tell me where you got that little thought from.'

'You need to trust me, Paddy. Matilda has visions. She sees them in her emerald pram.'

Paddy grabbed his car keys. Who was he to spoil a girl's dreams? Was Matilda some kind of a witch? He'd often wondered why she'd chosen a shamrock necklace for Tallulah. Still, a bit of a helping hand was always welcome. 'Come along then, if you insist, I'll take you to a pub. I was planning on having a night in, but what a girl wants, a girl gets.'

23

THE PINT OF GUINNESS

Paddy parked his car and opened the door for Tallulah to step out. 'Oh, it's so beautiful here. Shall we try to find the perfect field for me to run around before we buy a pint?'

Paddy grinned. 'I think that's the best idea you've had all day. I'm up for a little stroll. There's a bench near the lake where we can sit down and take in the view. You'll have plenty of fields to choose from around here.'

The couple walked hand in hand. 'Do you really have a soft spot for me? You did say that earlier, didn't you? I wasn't dreaming, was I? Wait a minute – why is there a pint of Guinness on that bench over there?'

'To be sure that's a lot of questions. I can only remember the last one. The Guinness will be for me; I'm a regular at the pub; they know I like to sit on that bench.'

Tallulah ran over to the bench and picked up the pint. 'I've got it! Now I need to run around with it.'

Paddy jogged over to join her. 'Woah! Let me have a few sips first. I don't want you bringing me back an empty glass.' Paddy sat down and gestured for Tallulah to join him.

Tallulah racked her brain. Did Matilda say if the glass was empty or full? It was important to get it right. Yes, that was it! Matilda said that she saw Tallulah running through a field with a pint glass. She said it was very green with lots of trees. She didn't mention any beer in the glass. Come to think of it; it would be silly to run around with a full glass. Tallulah suppressed the thought that it would also be absurd running around a field with an empty glass. Why would she even consider it? Why was she clinging onto a stupid vision? Paddy must think she was mad.

Paddy took his time drinking the pint. He seemed deep in thought. Tallulah sat rigid with her hands in her lap. She'd blown it. Paddy didn't even confirm that he had a soft spot for her; he avoided the question. She'd only been in Ireland for a few hours, and Paddy had realised that she was just a walking disaster.

Paddy finished his drink and handed the pint glass to Tallulah. 'I'm sure there's a bit of magic about in the mountains. Look what I've found at the bottom of the most delicious pint of Guinness I've ever tasted.'

Tallulah peered into the glass. 'It's a key charm.'

Paddy took a handkerchief out of his pocket and dried the charm before giving it to Tallulah. 'You can put it on your necklace with the shamrock if you like.'

Tallulah frowned as she threaded the key onto the chain. Paddy was up to something, and she couldn't work out what.

'Why didn't you answer any of my calls? It took me ages to find the card you gave to Bruce. But when I finally got your number, I couldn't get hold of you. You were in the pub with Miss Mae, weren't you? Don't try to lie. Miss Mae noticed I'd been calling you and she called me back.'

Paddy smiled. 'Now, in the line of work I'm in, I have more than one phone.' Paddy reached into his pocket. 'This is the phone I have been using this week, and there are no missed calls from you.'

Tallulah raised an eyebrow. 'That leads me to my next question: What exactly is your job?'

'Private surveillance. It pays well and takes me all over the world.'

'Isn't it dangerous, though? What do your family think about it?'

Paddy looked at Tallulah, and she noticed the brightness in his eyes diminish. 'I have no family. My parents were killed in a case of mistaken identity when I was four.'

'Oh, Paddy, I'm so sorry to hear that.'

Paddy squeezed Tallulah's hand. 'It's not a problem. I've just had to become self-sufficient. It's not a bad thing.'

Tallulah jumped up and retrieved the empty pint glass. 'Excuse me for a moment while I run around this field.'

Paddy grinned. Tallulah was one of a kind; he'd never met anyone quite like her. Tallulah's long curly red hair flew behind her as she ran through the grass with the pint glass in her hand. When she returned to the bench, her cheeks were flushed, and her eyes sparkled.

'There! I've carried out Matilda's vision. Let's go into that pub and celebrate. There's smoke coming from the chimney; it'll be cosy inside.'

It certainly was cosy inside; it was tiny. Paddy waved to the leprechaun sitting in the corner, and Tallulah burst out laughing. 'It's him! The one who picked me up from the airport. Now, wait a minute, who made up the story about my services being required in a rubbish pub in Dublin?'

Paddy's eyes twinkled. 'To be sure, there are no rubbish pubs in Dublin. That was Miss Mae's idea. She tracked me down yesterday morning to give me my spare phone back. Your father's quite good at spinning a yarn too.'

Tallulah gulped. 'You were in Truelove Hills yesterday, and you didn't come to see me?'

Paddy winked. 'That's correct. I thought it was time for you to come to see me. I know everything about you; now we need to even up the playing field. It won't take long; you'll soon realise that I'm just a simple soul. What you see is what you get.'

Tallulah threw her arms around him and squeezed as tightly as she could. 'There's nothing simple about you, Paddy. You're the most exciting man I've ever met.'

Paddy stood at the bar, and Tallulah took a seat at a table near the fire. The leprechaun soon joined her. 'I see it worked then.' Tallulah frowned, and the leprechaun continued, 'You're thrilled to bits now that Paddy's given you the key to his heart.'

24

CONFESSIONS AT THE CHATEAU

One week later, Tabitha arrived at the chateau armed with flowers. Lady Leticia Lovett had invited her for a "girls' afternoon", which would also include Miss Mae.

Tabitha's conscience still pricked about the matchmaking event turning into such a disaster. As it turned out, Miss Mae was streetwise and not averse to a trick or two, but Lady Leticia had innocently tried her best to bring romance into Tabitha and Tallulah's lives. Who could have known that true love didn't need a helping hand – it just happened naturally.

Leticia sat on a sofa surrounded by a mountain of clothes. 'I've decided to have a clear out. Tabitha should be able to squeeze into some of my dresses, and I'm sure Miss Mae could upgrade her wardrobe with the odd hat or shawl.'

Miss Mae picked up a pair of gold sandals. 'Size four! These will be perfect for me.'

Tabitha admired the embroidery on an exquisite lilac satin ballgown. 'This is so beautiful, Lady Leticia.'

'Oh, that one. It is rather lovely, isn't it? I wore that dress the evening I met my late husband.'

Miss Mae was busy matching up shoes to bags and had now salvaged six sets.

Tabitha was intrigued. 'Tell me about your late husband, Lady Leticia. Was he living in the chateau when you met him? Did he come from a rich family?'

A serenity encompassed Lady Leticia as she recalled her youth. 'I was very young when I met Lord Lionel Lovett at a Valentine's Ball in London. He was a lot older than me, very sophisticated, and I was entranced. He was a property developer. We spent our first years together living in a penthouse apartment a stone's throw from Buckingham Palace. When Lionel retired, he bought this chateau, and we moved from the city to the country.'

Tabitha folded the clothes into neat piles. There wasn't anything she would choose to wear. She may just take a few things to appease the Lady. 'If it's all right with you, Lady Leticia, could I please take these dresses? There are some in this pile that I'm sure Tallulah would like.'

Leticia's mind sprang back to the present. 'Now, where did you say Tallulah's gone to again?'

Miss Mae flung a pink feather boa around her neck. 'Ireland. Tallulah's popped over to Ireland. She could be gone a while.'

Tabitha chuckled. 'Tallulah's run off to be with Paddy.'

Leticia dropped an armful of clothes onto the floor. 'Not the long-haired Irish bachelor that listed his occupation as "a bit of this and that"?'

Miss Mae nodded. 'That's the one. It appears that Tallulah's shamrock necklace caught his eye. How weird was that? Out of all the necklaces in Matilda's shop and she gave Tallulah a shamrock. Funny how things turn out.'

Leticia huffed. 'Well, I hope that girl's thought things through.'

Miss Mae puffed up the feathers around her neck. 'Oh, I'm sure she has. Tabitha, please come with me into the cloakroom. I want to see if this shade of pink matches my complexion. There's a very good mirror in there.'

With the cloakroom door shut, Miss Mae changed the subject. 'I don't want this feather boa – pink ages me. I was just keen to enquire how things are going between you and Will Tomlin?'

Tabitha beamed. 'They couldn't be better, Miss Mae. You'll never guess what?'

'What?'

'Will didn't have a Caribbean holiday booked after all. He said it was just a little white lie to attract my attention. He's offered to book one now, but we both agree we'd much rather rent a cottage in Cornwall than jet off to the other side of the world.'

Miss Mae did a little jig. 'That's wonderful news, Tabitha! Does Leticia know about you and Will?'

'No, not yet. Will's going to have to tell her soon though because she's planning a matchmaking event just for him before she runs off on a world cruise with Gerard. Oops, that's a secret. Please don't tell anyone.'

Miss Mae squeezed her hands together in delight. 'Well, I never. So that's why she's having a clear-out; she's got a new man! Of course, I'll keep it a secret. I'm full of those. I never let one out.'

There was a knock on the cloakroom door. 'What are you two doing in there? I've just asked Gerard to carry down my selection of fur coats. I'll only be needing one or two for where I'm going.'

Miss Mae winked at Tabitha and hugged her. 'I'm so pleased things have worked out for you and Will.'

At the end of the afternoon, and armed with two large bags of accessories, Miss Mae spun around in the courtyard of the chateau before stopping to admire the cascading replica of the Trevi Fountain. Now, there was an idea. Miss Mae had never been to Rome. Maybe she should head there for her next big adventure? Yes, Miss Mae had a good feeling – her next stop would be Rome.

Gerard interrupted Miss Mae's thoughts by pushing a package into one of her bags. 'It's just a little treat for you, Miss Mae, to thank you for suggesting the world cruise. I would never have thought of that myself.'

25

TIME FOR CHANGE

Tallulah had been in Ireland for four weeks when the invitation dropped through the letterbox. 'Paddy! Miss Mae's leaving Truelove Hills and she's invited us to a party in the King Arthur before she goes.'

Paddy read the invitation. 'A week on Saturday. Perfect timing! I can always rely on Miss Mae.'

Tallulah pushed Paddy onto the sofa and held him down with a firm hand on his chest. 'And what do you mean by that? Are you planning on my stay being over in a week? I suppose you'll be buying me another one-way ticket.'

Paddy ran his fingers through Tallulah's hair. He loved the way the colour changed when the sun shone on it and the way it fell into a natural abundance of curls. In fact, he loved a lot about Tallulah.

'I've been doing some serious thinking recently. It's been grand having you over here for a holiday, but I need to earn a living.'

Tallulah's heart sank. She wanted them to stay cocooned in the Wicklow Mountains. She wanted to go for long walks every day, stop off at quaint pubs for lunch and come home to the glass-fronted mountain house with magnificent views of the Irish countryside. She wanted to cook dinner for Paddy every night and for him to make breakfast every morning. She didn't want much; she just wanted Paddy.

Paddy sensed her unease. 'We still have another week, and then we need to get back to reality. We can't live like this forever.'

*

Two days' later, Paddy rushed out of the house to take a call. Tallulah was suspicious. When he returned, she confronted him. 'Who was on the phone?'

'Now that would be telling.'

'You told me that you're a "simple soul" and that "what you see is what you get". You can't have secrets from me, Paddy. It's just not fair.'

'Well, all I will say is that I've got some business going on and it means we need to go to Truelove Hills a bit earlier than planned.'

'When do we need to go?'

'Tomorrow.'

*

When the door of the King Arthur flew open, and Tallulah breezed in, there were cheers from the regulars. Tabitha dashed over to embrace her twin. 'How was Ireland? How was Paddy? You need to tell me everything.'

'Well, Ireland was green. Very green. A leprechaun picked me up from Dublin airport. I ran around a field with a pint glass as Matilda predicted, and I had a wonderful month with Paddy, until now.'

Tabitha held her sister at arm's length. 'What do you mean "until now"? Why have you got a key charm next to your shamrock?'

Tallulah felt Bruce Copperfield's eyes boring into the side of her head. 'If you help me upstairs with my bags, we can have a chat in my room.'

Sitting on Tallulah's bed, Tabitha reached over to get a better look at her sister's new charm. 'Go on, tell me how you got this. Did Paddy buy it for you?'

'It turned up at the bottom of a pint of Guinness, and the leprechaun fooled me into believing it was the key to Paddy's heart. For clarification, it was the same leprechaun who picked me up from the airport.'

Tabitha giggled. 'Wow! It sounds like you've had some fun. Where's Paddy now and why are you in a strop with him? You can't fool me. I know when you're in a bad mood.'

'Well, Paddy's up to something. He dropped me off here in a taxi and said he had to "get on with some business". He's been acting strange the last few days. I thought I knew everything about him. He certainly knows everything about me.'

Tabitha squeezed her sister's hand. 'Well, anyway, I'm so pleased you're back. I have lots of news of my own to fill you in on, but it'll need to wait until later. I must get back downstairs before Bruce's blood pressure goes through the roof. If you and Paddy are an item, then we'll need to find a distraction for Bruce or working in the pub together won't be very pleasant.'

*

Hannah had been busy working around the clock to draw up contracts following phone calls from Lady Leticia Lovett and Lord Clive Sonning-Smythe earlier in the week. She had two meetings booked for this afternoon. The first was with Lady Lovett and Will Tomlin.

The lady crossed her legs to the side and sat with

her hands in her lap. She was keen to get this done so that she could get away on her cruise. Will Tomlin looked like a rabbit in the headlights.

Hannah gestured to Leticia to speak. 'I was made aware last year that you, Will, are a direct descendant of the original Lord at the chateau. To put it simply, your great-grandmother, who was a housekeeper, had an affair with the Lord. When the Lord's wife found out they sold the property. It was left to rack and ruin before my late husband bought it and I used my talents to renovate it. As I do not have any family to leave the chateau to, I feel it only right and proper that I leave it to you.'

Will tried not to slide off his chair. He gripped the edges of it with both hands and barely registered Leticia's words as she continued.

'As I am shortly off on a world cruise, I thought it would be a good time to sign the chateau over. I want to enjoy my latter years. Running a house and business no longer excites me. I am also comforted that you have taken up with a very nice young girl. Tabitha has always been my preference to Tallulah.'

Hannah raised one eyebrow and suppressed a grin as she handed Will a pen. 'Please read the contract carefully, Will, and if you are in agreement, sign on the dotted line.'

*

Hannah's second meeting involved Clive and Paddy. Paddy signed the contract, and Clive handed him the keys. 'I must say that I can't quite believe how spot-on the timing has been for the release of my hillside properties. I hope you and Tallulah will both be very happy living in the hills adjacent to Pebble Peak.'

Paddy shook hands with Clive. 'I'm sure we will, Clive. I'm sure we will.'

After Clive had left Hannah's office, Paddy rubbed his hands together and winked at Hannah. 'Now, Hannah, do you have another contract for me to sign?'

Hannah produced the documents. 'This has been a brilliant idea of Miss Mae's. It's a win-win situation for me. Expanding my law firm to include the services of a Private Investigator makes perfect sense. Welcome to the team, Paddy!'

26

SECRETS REVEALED

Tabitha was shocked. 'Lady Leticia has signed the chateau over to you?'

Will paced around the kitchen of his house in the grounds of the chateau. 'She certainly has, and it's all thanks to my great-grandmother having an affair with the Lord who had funny eyes. My grandfather had the same eyes and my father. If they were alive now, they'd be horrified.'

Tabitha laughed. 'Well, let's be thankful for small mercies. As the only remaining Tomlin, you can keep your great-grandmother's secret.'

Will continued to pace. 'What am I going to do, Tabitha? I'm an accountant, not a Lord.'

Tabitha sat down and held her head in her hands.

'Let me think. For it to work, you will need a good team behind you. You'll need to give up your job at the vineyard. Toby can recruit a new accountant and just the fact that you *are* an accountant means you will easily keep on top of the finances here. One of the first jobs will be to appoint a new butler as Gerard's running off into the sunset with Lady Leticia. The next thing will be to recruit a General Manager, someone who's used to working in the hospitality trade.'

Will stood with hands on hips. 'I've got it! You could be my General Manager. The position will, of course, include accommodation and I'll pay you a good salary.'

Tabitha's eyes widened. 'Do you think I could do it?'

'Of course. I'll help you. You can go on a training course. Whatever it takes. We can do this together.'

Tabitha squealed with delight. 'OK, then! Just wait until Tallulah hears about this!'

*

At seven o'clock, Paddy strode into the pub and headed straight to the bar. 'I need a can of Guinness and a glass. I've come for my woman.'

Tallulah pushed a glass and a can towards Paddy, and he grabbed her hand. 'Come with me, Miss

Makepeace.'

Tallulah giggled all the way up the High Street to the top of Pebble Peak. 'Where are you taking me? It's dark up here.'

Paddy switched on a torch and searched for a suitable stone to sit on next to the lake. He patted the space next to him, and Tallulah sat down too. He handed her a key. 'You see those houses over there in the hills? What do you think of the one with the lights on?'

Tallulah screwed up her face and tried to focus on the house while Paddy opened the can of Guinness and poured it into the glass. 'It looks lovely. It's not dissimilar to your house in the Wicklow Mountains. Why have you given me this key?'

Paddy sipped his Guinness. 'Now that would be telling. Let's just say for now that I've bought the house, but it comes with a condition attached.'

Tallulah sat in stunned silence as Paddy shone the torch around the field at the top of Pebble Peak and over to the house with the lights on. When he finished his pint, he turned the torch off and took hold of her hand. They sat together in the dark.

Paddy spoke first. 'You would never believe it, but there's magic in these hills. In fact, Tallulah Makepeace, I am coming to the conclusion that wherever you are, there's magic. You've certainly cast a spell on me.'

Paddy turned the torch on again and handed Tallulah the pint glass. 'Look what's at the bottom of my pint this time.'

Tallulah screamed! 'It's a ring!' She tipped it out and handed it to Paddy. 'Don't bother wiping it, just put it on my finger before you change your mind. There's something I need to do.'

Paddy placed the ring on Tallulah's finger, and she grabbed the pint glass before running around the field with the just the light from Paddy's torch guiding her way. Paddy laughed. 'Come back here, you mad woman. You need to seal our engagement with a kiss.'

*

By the time the morning of Miss Mae's leaving party came around, there were two new barmaids in the King Arthur. Miss Mae had chosen them herself and Bruce and Steve's work rate had doubled. David Makepeace was grateful for her support. 'You once asked me, Miss Mae, what my deepest worries were and now, all of a sudden, they've vanished. There's something special about you, since you've been in Truelove Hills everything's fallen into place.'

Miss Mae pecked David on the cheek and thrust an envelope into his hand. 'I'm pleased to have been of assistance. There's enough money in there to make it a free bar tonight. Don't you go opening it until the end of the evening.'

David nodded, and Miss Mae waved as she left the pub.

During the afternoon, the Makepeace girls (including the heavily pregnant Hannah) blew up balloons, tied bunting to the rafters and unravelled the large poster portraying a photograph of Miss Mae doing one of her jigs. Tears streamed down Matilda's face. 'She's going to love this one. What are we going to do without her?'

Clive and Arthur helped to polish glasses behind the bar while the decorations were being hung. Arthur poured two secret pints. 'Let's keep these between us, Clive. David will never know.'

Clive turned to face the wall and took a crafty sip of beer before winking at Arthur. 'I tell you what, Arthur. Miss Mae has got me thinking differently. Life's not worth living if you don't have some fun. That woman's a whirlwind. She's brought far more to the lives of everyone in Truelove Hills than she can ever imagine.'

By eight o'clock the pub was heaving. David Makepeace had compiled a music playlist to suit Miss Mae's personality: it was fun, loud, and . . . well, just fun and loud. The free bar was much appreciated and by nine o'clock everyone was singing, dancing and making merry.

It wasn't until ten o'clock that David Makepeace noticed that Miss Mae hadn't turned up. He rang her phone – which was switched off. He asked Clive to go to Villa Elena in case she'd been taken ill and, when that proved unsuccessful, he requested the services of Paddy to find her.

By eleven o'clock, there was still no sign of Miss Mae. David reached for the envelope she had given him that morning. He ripped it open to the sight of a huge wad of cash, and a letter:

Dear David

I hope my leaving party went well. I am not good with goodbyes.

Harriet will be proud of the man you've become. A fine figure I might add.

Yours truly

Mirabelle Mae

David wiped away a tear. He hoped that Harriet would be proud of him, that was all he'd ever wanted. He folded the letter and put it in his pocket before turning off the music and making an announcement to the partying crowd.

'On behalf of Miss Mae, I would like to thank you all for coming to her leaving party. It is our loss that she wasn't able to be here herself.'

David raised his half-empty glass of beer. 'I would like to propose a toast . . . to Miss Mae.'

*

The bed on the train was quite comfortable. Miss Mae was pleasantly surprised. The overnight sleeper to London and then an afternoon flight to Rome. What more could a girl want? She had no idea why her destiny was taking her to Italy, but she was going to have fun finding out. Miss Mae smiled as she pulled the bed covers up under her chin before drifting off to sleep.

EPILOGUE

Two days later, Miss Mae sat on the stone steps opposite the Trevi Fountain. She was grateful for her ample padding; late autumn in Italy wasn't the warmest place to be. Yet, with one of the world's finest gelaterias within arm's reach, it would be a crime not to sit on a cold step eating an authentic gelato.

'Miss Mae! What are you doing in my homeland? I am in big fear, and I need your services.'

The sight of bachelor Giovanni, with a full set of teeth, made Miss Mae chuckle. 'Giovanni! How lovely to see you. I am just passing by on my travels, what a coincidence bumping into you.'

'I mean it, Miss Mae. I need your services.'

The gelato in Miss Mae's hand was starting to melt, and she licked it with speed.

'Since you suggested I got my teeth fixed, there is a queue of girls outside my palazzo in Venice. I have no idea who to choose. I need your help.'

'I take it you will pay well?'

'Of course, and you can stay in my palazzo for free. I need you, Miss Mae. You're the Matchmaker.'

'When's the next flight to Venice? Or is it best to travel by train? I suppose we'll need to get on a boat for the last part and sail down the Grand Canal. Any chance you could make it a gondola?'

'There is a high-speed train in two hours. I will arrange for my private gondola to collect us at Santa Lucia station.'

Miss Mae held out her sticky hand to shake Giovanni's. 'It's a deal, Giovanni. It's a deal!'

****

Printed in Great Britain
by Amazon